"IN NOMINE BEZEMOTH"

He broke a branch from a tree and used it to draw a circle around the dog's skeleton. Then he piled damp forest earth onto the bones until he had built a mound of mud. As he worked, he chanted: *"In nomine Bezemoth Ipsissimus levo hic spiritus . . ."*

The mound of the mud began to steam and quiver.

"Ratam, rationablem, accetabliemque facere digneris."

The mud smoothed itself, grew black hair like grass. Eyes bulged behind newly formed lids; damp nostrils quivered.

"In nomine Bezemoth."

The dog moved a leg. Showed it teeth. Opened an eye. The eye was red, demonically red.

The Fair Rules of Evil

DAVID C. SMITH

AVON BOOKS · NEW YORK

AVON BOOKS
A division of
The Hearst Corporation
105 Madison Avenue
New York, New York 10016

First Avon Books Printing: April 1989

For LAURIE,
who read it first
and was frightened

Thou shalt not be afraid for the terror by night; nor for the arrow that flieth by day; nor for the pestilence that walketh in darkness; nor for the destruction that wasteth at noonday.

Psalms 91:5–6

Part I

DAVID TREVISAN

A week before his sister was found, David Trevisan decided to leave the seminary.

He was in Cincinnati, a long way from home, and he'd made a serious mistake in coming here and he couldn't deny it anymore, couldn't rationalize it anymore. Looking for something that should've been inside himself but wasn't, looking for it in the safety of the church. And it wasn't there, not for him.

Several times in the past few months he'd tried to work up the courage to go to Father Kendrick and tell him, but he'd always talked himself out of it. Now it wasn't courage; it was pride. Guilt, perhaps, but pride, certainly. He didn't belong here with these other young men who believed fervently and wished to devote their lives to what they believed in.

David didn't know what he believed in.

Father Kendrick saw him on a Friday afternoon.

David liked Father Kendrick; all of them did. He was a sympathetic man, rare in this world. Busy, true, and a politician, of course. But a sincerely good man, and David hadn't known very many sincerely good people in his life.

David sat in front of Father Kendrick's desk. The office was warm, all wood. Father Kendrick took his time. He made small talk for a few minutes.

Then he said, "I knew it when you walked in here."

"Did you?"

"Young men . . . when they come here at first, they

have a look in their eyes. You have the other look, David. I'm sorry to see it."

"I'm sorry, too, Father."

"How have we failed you?"

"I don't think you've failed me, Father. Maybe I've failed you."

"You've been here—what? About a year?"

"Yes."

"And doing very well. Excellent grades."

"Thank you."

"You came here after your parents died."

"That's right."

He referred to the file on his desk. "They were killed in a car accident."

"Yes."

"Do you feel that their deaths had something to do with your turning to the church?"

"Yes, Father, I do."

"You considered entering the seminary because you felt—confused after the accident?"

"I don't think I really wanted to become a priest," David told him. "I think I just wanted to hide for a while. Not a good reason for becoming a priest, is it?"

"No. No, I'm afraid not." Father Kendrick smiled. "But your instincts were right."

"Has it happened before?"

"Oh, yes."

"Often?"

Father Kendrick shrugged. "You're how old?"

"Twenty-six. Just turned twenty-six."

"I can give you time to think about this."

"Thank you, but—I have been thinking about it."

"I want you to feel that my door is always open to you."

"Thank you, Father Kendrick."

"You'll have some papers to sign."

"I understand."

"What do you intend to do?"

"I don't know yet. Find an apartment, maybe a job. Maybe go back to Noland. My sister, Ginny. We have the house our parents left us. Money."

"Do you have any work in mind?"

"Not at the moment, no, sir."

"I want you to feel that Christ is with you, David."

"Thank you, Father. I'll try."

"Don't you believe in Christ? Don't you feel that Christ is with you?"

"This is . . . very uncomfortable for me, Father."

He moved into a little two-room walk-up with a bath in downtown Cincinnati, not sure yet that he wanted to go home. He wanted to wait for the seminary to get the paperwork cleared up; he'd turned over some assets and those would have to be returned.

David wasn't worried about money. He and Ginny had money.

But what was he going to do with himself?

He phoned her the night he moved in.

"Gin? How're you doing?"

"Okay, I guess." Munching on something. "Long time no hear."

"I know, I know. Is everything okay?"

"Sure."

"I'm thinking of coming back."

"If you want."

"I don't know, I've been thinking about it. Maybe I'll come back."

"You okay?"

"Yeah, I'm okay. I guess I just miss you."

"I miss you, too."

"How's Cheryl?"

"She's okay."

"You see much of her?"

"Now really. Not for a while. I don't know, she's been acting funny."

"Gin, you know—"

"David, can I call you back? I gotta go."

"Sure. Okay."

"I'm sorry, I'll call you back. This friend of mine, he's coming over, I think he's here."

"No problem."

"Love you, big bro."

"I love you, too, Gin."

He'd done it. He'd fucked it up. He'd run away from it a year ago and that meant he'd run away from his sister, he might as well have abandoned her. He'd done it.

God, God, God . . .

A boy found her.

He was maybe twelve, thirteen years old. Carrying his .22 over one shoulder, on the lookout for rabbit. Tall Ohio grass in the summertime, sweat and flakes of grain and dust itching his forehead, canteen at his side, his dog running ahead of him, enjoying it all.

The dog let him know.

"What'd you find, Bob? What is it, boy?"

The dog stopped dead, looked back at him, sat, and began to moan. Looked up. At what? Moaned in that low-pitched, whining voice dogs sometimes get.

The dog jumped up suddenly and barked, loped half backward and, with his head turned to one side, whined.

The boy came running.

"What is it, Bob? What is it?"

And saw her.

Lying naked in the field. A woman. A blond, pudgy woman, naked. Curled up in the center of a ring of melted candles. Thirty, thirty-five candles.

"Jesus!"

Dead?

"Quiet, Bob, quiet!"

Muttering, barely above a whisper.

"Ite . . . ite ad locus . . . vestrum . . . Ite . . ."

The boy knelt down beside her. An older woman, in her twenties.

"Hey, miss? Miss?"

"Ite . . . ite ad locus . . ."

"Hey, miss, wake up. You okay?"

She opened her eyes, looked right at him.

"Miss?"

And screamed.

The boy's mother called the police.

By late in the morning the girl had been taken to Noland County Memorial, and the police were warning passersby in cars and trucks and the boy who'd found her and his buddies to keep back, stay out of the field, Jesus Christ, that's all we need is to have a bunch of yokels tromping around out here kicking things up.

Officers and detectives crouched in the field and looked for clues, not that their hearts were in it, tracking down some girl who was probably a runaway or some drug addict, sleeping in a field with a bunch of candles.

"Esposito said it looks like some kind of witchcraft."

"He oughta know. His wife's a witch."

"Tell him to his face."

"I've told him to his face. I've told *her* to her—"

"No sign of drugs?"

"No sign of drugs."

"That don't mean shit."

"Found her car."

"You find some *clothes*?"

"She look blue to you? She looked blue."

"Blue . . ."

"Got cold last night."

"Didn't get that cold. It's fucking September."

"So do we know who she is?"

"Trevaysan. Trevisan. Virginia R. Trevisan. Trevisan."

"That's who the car belongs to."

"April fourteenth . . . She's twenty-three. This girl look twenty-three to you?"

"Virginia R. Trevisan. Running Brook Drive. Nice neighborhood."

"So nice kids do drugs, too."

"Call her parents?"

"Nothing yet."

"You mean the fucking parents don't know she's out here all night doing drugs in a field?"

He'd decided to go back home.

He had his clothes packed—not that he'd ever really unpacked when he'd moved from the seminary dorm. David didn't own a great deal, anyway. A small wardrobe, books, pictures of his parents and his sister.

It was a Saturday and storming. Thunder boomed and rattled the windows a little, the raindrops hitting hard. Mindful little things attacking the glass.

He took down the crucifix above his bureau and dropped it on top of the clothes neatly folded in his open suitcase on the bed. And from the top of the bureau he took down the framed color photo of his sister Ginny and dropped it, too, on top of the clothes in the suitcase.

In the kitchen, the telephone rang.

As David went to answer it, thunder boomed loudly.

"Yes. Yes, this is David Trevisan. Virginia, yes—Ginny. What happened? What?"

Thunder boomed again.

In the open suitcase, the glass cracked in the framed photo of his sister.

"No, I understand. Yes, I understand." Numb, crazy.

"I'll come back. Yes. Give me—give me four hours. I don't know. Five hours."

He finished packing in a daze. Got in his car and drove. Just drove.

Stopped outside Columbus early in the afternoon because he had to fill the car, angry with the minutes that held him back. Just wanting to know. Just needing to know.

Mile after mile of freeway, David speeding up when a line of cars deliberately slowed him down, calming down when he spotted a highway patrol car.

The sun was going down when he reached the outskirts of Noland. Little dinosaur factory town. Dead.

Dead . . .

If she wasn't dead when they found her, was she dead now? Had they lied to him? Just to stop him from going crazy?

What if she were dead?

What had he done to her, what would he do if she were dead?

It was a private room. His father, a solitary man, must have put that in the insurance because he would have preferred it himself.

Cheryl looked up when David came in. He'd expected her to be there. She was sitting by the bed, and she stood up in slow motion, facing him, all dark hair and eyes, as pretty as ever. Staring at him. With the same hurt, surprised look on her face as when he'd left her a year ago with: Look, I'm not comfortable with this but I feel I have to do it, just let me do it, I think this is what I need.

"Oh, David, I'm so sorry! I don't know what to tell you!"

And then Ginny, as Cheryl, hovering, stepped aside. Ginny, lying there, pale even for her, the dirty blond hair fallen back from her forehead, eyes closed, an IV in her arm.

David looked at Cheryl again. She was right there and she threw her arms around him and hugged him. He felt her, not quite real.

"I don't know what to tell you!"

"Cheryl . . . What happened?"

She led him to the bed and let him go, and David leaned over his sister.

"Ginny? Hey, Gin, I'm here. It's David."

"They found her in a field, did they tell you that?"

"Yes."

"Oh, David, I don't know what she was doing out there! It's scary. It's scary."

He turned around. "What's scary?"

She shook her head.

David looked from Cheryl to the woman coming through the door. Nurse.

"David Trevisan?"

No, a doctor.

"Yes."

They went down the hall to the sunroom, deserted at this time of night, where they could talk privately. Low voices.

"This is all happening too fast for me," David said.

Dr. Marquette lit a cigarette, looked him in the eyes. She had very deep eyes. Not like Father Kendrick's.

"Your sister's not comatose. It's kind of a state of shock. We don't know what triggered it. And frankly, we can't reach her."

"She was found naked in a field."

"She wasn't molested. There're no signs of molestation. You understand what I'm saying?"

"She wasn't raped."

"She wasn't raped. You know your sister better than we

do. You can tell us more than we can tell you, at this point. Can I call you David? David, she was found inside a kind of ring of melted candles. She was naked and she was wearing strange jewelry.''

''You make it sound like some kind of witchcraft.''

''You tell me.'' Dr. Marquette blew smoke. ''Is that your sister? Things like that?''

''I don't know. We haven't seen much of each other for the past year.''

''She did herself a great deal of harm out there.''

''How long does she have to stay here?''

''Until we can—''

''Can I take her home?''

''Out of the question. If she comes out of this—when she comes out of this—then we can make a determination. Right now your sister is completely withdrawn from the world.''

He drove out to the field. It was nearly dark and Cheryl went with him.

He parked his car off the side of the road. Gravel country road in the middle of nowhere. No city in sight, just field, grass, trees.

Cheryl held back a little but followed him as David walked through the tall grass, crickets chirping all around. He came to where they'd found her, the grass tramped down now, tire tracks crushing the weeds.

There were still signs of melted candles. There was a circle, twelve, maybe fifteen feet across, outlined by the candles. It looked sinister.

''Why?'' David asked, kneeling down.

Cheryl wrapped her arms around herself.

They didn't see it from where they were in the field but behind them, back on the road, another car pulled to a slow, quiet stop behind David's. It had out-of-state plates— New York.

The driver watched them, David and Cheryl, two shadows out there in the darkness. Black man dressed in an old, worn trenchcoat. As he watched them he rested his elbow out the open driver's window.

He didn't have a left hand.

"Do you know?" David fingered the candle wax in the grass. "Do you know what she was trying to do, Cheryl?"

"I think you and I better go back and have a talk."

The black man eased his car into reverse, coasted back behind the cover of some low trees, moved ahead quietly, tires barely crunching on the gravel.

"She was just very quiet. She didn't go out. Weeks would go by. Months. She just never called. I'd see her in the grocery store or something."

"She said you were the one who was acting funny."

"Me? When did she say that?"

"I called her . . . last week. Shit."

They were sitting in the kitchen David had grown up in. Like someone else's house, now. Not even any ghosts or memories here. A kitchen.

Cheryl had made coffee, knowing where things were in the cupboards and drawers, knowing how to operate the coffee maker Ginny must have bought.

"It's because of Mom and Dad," David said, feeling it. What had he done? "I went away . . . It's like I was abandoning her."

Cheryl reached a hand across the kitchen table, didn't quite reach his. David's hands were clenched. "You can't say that. I felt the same way but don't you say that. She wanted to be by herself. She changed."

"What do you mean, she changed?"

"I don't know. She changed."

"Have you changed?"

"David . . ."

"What about that boyfriend she had?"

"Oh, he moved to California. Last year."

"Then there was somebody else. She was seeing somebody. I know. She told me."

"Oh, God."

"What?"

"There's this man, he lectured at the college a few months ago. His name is Professor Fry. I only met him once. Gin mentioned him a couple of times. I think she was seeing him."

"What did he do to her?"

"He didn't 'do' anything to her. He just . . . Oh, David."

"What?"

"I hope this doesn't . . . I only met him once but I kind of introduced her to him."

"What about it, Cheryl?"

"All this stuff about candles and witchcraft? I think he turned her on to it."

"Great."

"He's an anthropologist or something."

She watched him. Very quiet. She finished the last of her coffee and got up and went to the sink, rinsed out the cup.

"You're not mad or anything, are you?"

He looked at her. "About what?"

"About me. Everything."

"God, no."

He saw Cheryl searching his eyes. David stood up and walked over to her. She leaned forward and embraced him and leaned her head on his chest, needing to.

"I just feel so bad about this. It just doesn't make sense."

"Well, we'll just look after each other, okay? We'll get through this." He put his arms around her.

"David, I'm afraid—I've been kind of waiting."

"Have you?"

"Stupid, huh?"

She looked up at him.

He told her carefully, "It was a mistake, Cheryl. I quit."

"When?"

"A week ago. Week and a half ago."

"Oh, David, why?"

"I went there so I wouldn't have to deal with things. That was the only reason. You knew that, you tried to tell me that."

"God, I'm so sorry."

"I'm no priest," David said.

They each had another cup of coffee and talked about different things, reminiscing. Cheryl's job at the real estate office. Some of the people David had known at the seminary.

But any topic they started wound up coming back, settling on them like a cloud, reminding them of where they were, the weight of it.

"Christ," David said. "It doesn't make any sense, does it? You can't plan on anything, you can't count on anything. You think you know what's going on, but you don't. You don't."

When Cheryl was ready to leave, yawning but fighting her tiredness, they walked quietly into the foyer, and Cheryl put on her coat and rested a hand on the doorknob.

"Call me tomorrow?"

"Okay."

"Or I'll call you. We'll go to the hospital."

"Okay."

"It's going to be fine."

"I guess."

"David?" Carefully. "Do you want me to stay?"

Slowly, he shook his head.

* * *

He called the hospital. Virginia R. Trevisan?

No, no change in her condition.

He took a shower but that didn't calm him down. Restless, he walked around the house, looking into the rooms from his childhood, straining to hear but not hearing familiar old sounds, old voices. He didn't cry. He didn't feel particularly sentimental. He was numb.

He'd come home.

He poured himself another cup of coffee but forgot it on the counter when he went up to his sister's room, feeling like an intruder, feeling guilty ahead of time.

She hadn't changed or rearranged anything much in the past year. David went to her bureau and tried not to recognize himself in the mirror as he opened several drawers, looked in, felt around the wooden box of jewelry, the belts, lifted up some underwear and blouses.

He knelt on the floor, looked under the bed, reached his hand under there, felt around. Some magazines. Shoes.

He went to the small bookcase by her desk, looked at the books, went through the drawers of her desk.

He swung open the closet doors, studied the floorful of shoes and shoeboxes, looked at the shelf overhead. Lots of boxes. Bags. He took some down. More shoes. A box of family photos. Another small stationery box with magazine and newspaper articles. Health, beauty, how to lose weight, vitamins, skin.

There was another box high on the shelf. David took it down and set it on the floor. He took out old college textbooks and notebooks—Ginny had tried off and on for a year to find something to concentrate on at Noland— and underneath these he found what he'd expected to find.

A dozen new candles, different colors, wrapped in tissue paper.

Three brass bowls of different sizes.

A dozen boxes of incense, different kinds.

A small decorative knife, probably bought at an import shop.

Three silver necklaces, chains with decorated coins on them. The coins were engraved with strange symbols.

And books. Books on witchcraft and magical rituals. Paperbacks. The covers bent and the spines cracked, with long paragraphs colored with yellow highlighter.

And a diary. One of those blank-paged books with pretty cloth covers. The first entry was dated almost a year ago. David was gone, she'd felt all alone and abandoned. There were entries every few days, sometimes a week apart.

After about twenty pages David read: "Cheryl + I to lecture. Prof. Fry. Cheryl doesn't really know him but met him once. I am ecstatic."

"Met and talked last night. He is wonderful! I think I have found the answer. David, you do it your way, I'll do it mine."

A few more entries. She and Fry and their talks about life and death, spirituality, God.

And then abruptly Ginny's handwriting was gone and in the same pen her entries were written in a code. In some kind of alphabet David had never seen before. Odd little letters or symbols, straight lines connected at angles like parodies of Roman letters, or Hebrew.

He couldn't read it.

Whatever she was saying here, whatever she'd done, whatever had happened between her last entry and David coming back home to find her lying comatose in a hospital bed—

He couldn't read it. There was no way of making the connection.

* * *

It was a large house set far back from the road. Long gravel driveway laid out like a gray ribbon, reaching over a small hill, snaking through some trees to take him to the wide parking area in front of the house.

Not a farmhouse, although it was surrounded by fields of grass and woods and nothing else in sight. Three stories. Luxurious in its day. Wide, long front porch, porticoed and pillared.

David parked his car and got out, squinted against the bright midmorning sun and walked up onto the porch. Knocked on the front door.

With his sister's diary in his left hand.

He looked around, a little nervous. The place hadn't been kept up. Bricks and stones out of alignment in the flower garden around the foundation of the house. Paint peeling. Some of the wooden trellis work badly in need of repair.

The front door opened.

"Professor Fry?"

"Yes." He was a tall shadow behind the screen door.

"I phoned the college. They told me you lectured there a few months ago."

"Who are you?"

"Oh. Sorry. David Trevisan."

"Her brother."

"That's right."

"The priest."

"Yes."

"I've spoken with the authorities already."

"I know that, sir."

David tried to see him through the screen door. He was hidden partly by the shadowed foyer. But he looked to be close to six feet tall, taller than David. Slim. Probably in his forties, but not showing any gray that David could see.

And with a presence. David felt it strongly—the kind of

commanding personality that intense, self-righteous persons have.

The screen door opened and Fry stepped back to let David in.

"Thank you."

Fry closed the door behind them. "May I take your jacket?"

"No, that's all right. I'll only be a few minutes."

"We'll go into the living room."

"All right."

The house was dimly lit. Fry led David down a side hallway, past a sunroom or enclosed porch and another closed room and into the living room.

All wood. Tall ceilings. Books everywhere. And on shelves on all the walls sat odd trophies and archaeological relics, porcelains and statuettes and figurines. There was a large fireplace, unlit. Two sofas and an old table. David had the sensation of going back in time, with the dim light and the heavy wooden furniture and all the books and odd ornaments. It was almost medieval.

The heavy drapes were drawn closed against the tall windows at the far end of the room.

Fry motioned for David to take a seat, so he moved to an old chair by the windows. Fry sat in a loveseat in the middle of the room.

He said, "My eyes are sensitive. An old injury. That's why the light. Now, then. Is she all right?"

"Ginny's still in some kind of coma. They're not sure what it is."

"I'm sorry to hear that."

"I'm just trying to piece together what might have happened."

"Do you think I can help?"

"I don't know. She was— They found her in a field. She was naked and she was surrounded by candles. Melted candles. It sounds like witchcraft or something."

"Magic," Fry told him. "Ritual magic."

"Black magic?"

"Well, ritual magic."

David edged forward in his chair. "Professor Fry, what do you think my sister was trying to do?"

"You mean, do I know what she was trying to do?"

"What do you think happened to her?"

"You're asking me if something supernatural happened to her."

"I don't know."

"Have you considered that?"

"Maybe. Maybe I am asking that."

"I see." Fry stood and put his arms behind his back, walked a few paces. "Your sister sat in on my lectures. She wasn't a student, and after a few weeks it became apparent to me what she was trying to do."

"And what was that?"

Fry told him, "I'm afraid I know more about you and your sister than you think I do."

David didn't care for that. "What did she tell you?"

"And about your parents."

"Do you?"

"I know how Ginny reacted to their deaths."

"She didn't accept it well at all."

"She denied it outright," Fry told him. "She couldn't accept it. Now I suspect that you yourself turned to the seminary for solace after they died. Am I right?"

"That's a little personal."

"Don't feel awkward about it. It's human nature. I was a divinity student myself at one time. But Ginny was attracted to me—I admit it—and she pestered me because she wanted to communicate with the spirit world. She wanted to talk to your dead parents."

It took David a moment. "What . . . did you do?"

"I'm not a psychiatrist; I'm a scholar. She's very emotional; she needed someone. She needed someone strong.

She wanted me to know her secrets, how guilty she felt. It was like a confession; she could've been a better daughter."

"She was angry with me."

"To a degree. I wasn't comfortable with it, but I can tell you honestly that I like Ginny."

"So what happened, precisely?"

Fry was very reassuring. "I went along with it because I thought it might help her work it out. But I told her that perhaps she ought to see a therapist. Someone on campus or at a clinic. She demurred."

"But what did you do? I mean, going along with her about this?"

"Candles and a seance. The Ouija board. Tarot cards. Humoring her."

"I see."

"I think I did the wrong thing," Fry admitted. "I didn't intend to plant anything in her mind. Eventually we argued and Ginny didn't come back."

"Do you know if she was seeing anyone else? Someone else who might have had some influence?"

"I really don't know."

"I found some books of hers," David told him. "Books on magic and witchcraft."

"I suspected as much."

"I found this, too." He stood up, holding it out. "It's a diary. But it's written in some kind of code."

Fry crossed the room and took it, opened it, glanced at the pages, riffling them.

"This isn't code," he said. "This is the Celestial Alphabet. It was used by all chemists. Medieval sorcerers and mystics."

"Can you read it?"

"Yes."

David watched him as Fry scanned a page, squinting a

little, turned the leaf and studied another page. He looked up.

"It's rather mundane, actually. A young woman's diary. It's a catalog of her feelings about your parents. Her experiments. Trying to contact the spirit world."

He handed the diary back to David. Their eyes met for a moment and held.

"I'm afraid," Fry said, "that she was a very unhappy young woman."

"So what do you think happened to her?"

Fry stepped away and swung his arms behind his back again. "I'm not a religious man but I'm a spiritual man. I've traveled and I've seen a great deal. I think she might have actually created something—conjured some spiritual force—and that the shock of it did this to her."

"Or—whatever it was that she conjured did this to her."

"There is that possibility," Fry admitted. "I think the universe is alive with many forces."

"Spirits?" David asked. "Demons?"

"Names. Call them what you will. I have an enormous respect for the invisible things that surround us. I think human beings are just one kind of spirit." He watched David. "That's not very consoling, is it?"

"Actually, I don't want to be consoled. I want to know what my sister did to herself."

"Well, then," Fry said. "Is there anything else?"

"No," David told him. "No, I suppose not."

In the foyer Fry rested his hand on the front doorknob and turned to him.

"I hope I've been of some help."

"I guess all I can do, quite honestly, is ask questions and wait to see what happens."

"I hope she'll be all right."

"Well, thanks very much for talking with me."

"Not at all."

Fry removed his hand from the doorknob and offered it; David took it. Again their eyes met.

And David thought he read something in Fry's look, but he dismissed it. Vague. A ripple.

Fry opened the door and David stepped through, then waited a moment on the porch.

"One last thing."

"What is it?"

"Did you and Ginny ever reach my parents?"

"I'm not precisely sure," Fry told him.

David nodded and went down the steps and got into his car.

Fry watched him go, listening as the engine started up, listening to the sound of tires on gravel, the noise of the car crunching slowly down the long driveway, the car itself disappearing over a low hill, appearing again as small as an insect down by the road, making its turn and going away.

Did he know, this priest?

Did he suspect?

Young man, asking questions. Young man himself searching for illumination, asking questions of God, writing poetry with his mind to the stars, wanting to know. Wanting to know.

All.

Fry closed the door and locked it. He moved through his dim house and went out the back door far at the other end, stepped onto the porch. Stood in the shadows of the low overhanging roof and looked out upon nature. Trees and grass and air and sun. Feeling it all as if it were an ocean and he submerged in it. Smelling the rocks and the trees, hearing the grass and the wind. The pulse of nature, alive.

He heard a fly buzzing, close by him on the porch.

Fry didn't look for the fly. He closed his eyes, took in

a deep breath, swallowed the air, and took it down deep into his belly. Exhaled. Inhaled again.

Did he know, this priest?

Did he suspect?

The fly continued to buzz, droning, oblivious, as Fry breathed, as Fry stood straight and tilted his head back.

Clenched his hands into tight fists.

Buzz.

As Fry listened. Began to murmur.

Buzz.

As Fry whispered.

Buzz.

As Fry's face reddened, the head tilting farther back.

Buzz—

As Fry whispered.

Whispered . . .

As the buzzing stopped.

Fry exhaled deeply. Opened his eyes. Shook his head and undid his fists.

There by his shoes on the floor of the wooden porch lay the fly. Dead.

The tall black man with no left hand was waiting for David Trevisan to arrive. When David came in, passing down the hospital hallway, the black man followed him with his eyes.

David turned into Ginny's room.

The black man got up from his chair in the waiting area and walked after him.

David was leaning over Ginny, sitting in a chair by the bed.

"Gin? How're you doing? It's me, it's David."

"Mr. Trevisan?"

He turned and looked up, startled.

"I wonder if I might have a word with you."

David rose, standing protectively by the bed. "Are you a doctor?"

Obviously he wasn't. The worn trenchcoat, the look, told David that. The whole attitude.

"No, I'm not a doctor. I'm an investigator."

"An investigator?"

"Retired police investigator. New York. Do you have a minute?"

"I suppose."

"What happened to your sister, here—it's similar to a series of crimes we had upstate."

"Who are you?"

"My name's Matthew Long. That doesn't mean anything to you, does it?"

"No . . . No." Some connection with Ginny?

"I'd like to talk to you."

"All right."

"Actually, I'd like to talk to your sister."

"My sister is comatose."

Long made no reply to that. He moved past David and sat down in the chair. David shot a glance toward the hospital room door.

He looked back at Long, noticing the missing left hand.

Long caught his eyes.

"An accident. Last year."

David thought it prudent to stay close; he stood behind the chair as Long seated himself.

Long leaned over Ginny intently, as if looking for clues or reasons David couldn't recognize.

"What kind of crimes in New York?" he asked.

Again Long didn't answer him but, hovering closely above Ginny, whispered in her ear, slowly and carefully.

"In nomine Agla Dominus et in nomine Bezemoth Ipsissimus—"

"That's Latin."

"—dirigatur, oratio mea—"

Ginny's brow furrowed. Her closed eyes tightened, the lids wrinkling. A tear squeezed from under one eye and dripped down her cheek.

"What're you saying to her, Mr. Long?"

"—sicut incensum. Non declinet—"

David put a heavy hand on Long's shoulder. "Is it a prayer?"

"—cor meum—"

As Ginny began to sob, choking a little, taking in a loud breath.

"Stop it! What're you doing?"

"—in verba malitiae—"

Ginny rolled onto her back, sobbing loudly and moving her arms. Waving her hands at something.

"Ginny! Stop it, Mr. Long!"

Long reached for her, and David's fingers, tightening, dug into his shoulder.

"I'm not hurting her, David!"

And Ginny began to yell. Her eyes opened and she screamed. "Ite! Ite in pace! Ad locus vestrum!"

"Jesus!" David let go of him and ran across the room to the door.

Long held on to Ginny as she began thrashing, yelling, fighting him and waving her arms.

"Ite! Ite!"

"Nurse! Doctor!" Leaning out the door, looking up and down the hall, the patients and nurses and nurses' aides staring at him, turning to stare at him. "Get someone! My sister's awake! Will you get someone?"

He looked back into the room. Ginny had quieted, sunk back on the bed, and Long was standing, looking down at her.

David ran back and pushed him roughly aside. "Ginny! Ginny!"

"Ite . . . oh, God . . . keep them—away . . ." Muttering. Staring. Tears still dripping, staring but not seeing. "Ite . . . ad locus . . ."

"What did you do to her?" he roared at Long.

Long didn't move.

David wanted to hit him, throw himself at him, as he looked Long in the eyes—

Like Fry's eyes.

A nurse rushed in. A big woman, her starchy uniform rustling and scraping like a web of tight skin.

"Oh, my God, she's out of it! Get away from her!" she yelled at Long. "Both of you! Get back!"

A second nurse ran in. Young and very frightened. "Oh, God, what—"

"Get Dr. Guffey! Get Dr. Guffey!"

The second nurse rushed out, flat heels clattering on the tile.

"Who are you?" The big nurse faced Long, her shadow waving ominously over Ginny's pale, sweating face.

"Police detective."

"No one gave you permission to come in here. You're both going to have to leave."

David said, "Look, I'd like to—"

"Please! Mr. Trevisan! Outside!"

David wasn't sure what to do. What if Ginny were dying, what if she wanted him there? Jesus, Jesus . . .

But Long, hunching his shoulders to readjust his coat, moved past him and crossed the room, waited in the doorway, and looked back.

So David followed him.

They went into the hallway and stood there, David trembling, as the young nurse hurried past, followed by an intern.

The door was closed.

David looked at Long but didn't say anything. He started down the hall, heading for the elevator.

He wasn't surprised that Long followed him.

They reached the little waiting area by the elevator doors and David pushed the down button. Long stepped up beside him.

David, not looking at him, asked, "Are you really the police, or what?"

"I was."

"What did you say to my sister? What was that?"

"Part of a magical ceremony."

The elevator doors opened.

"We need to talk, David."

David stepped inside the elevator, feeling cool all of a sudden. Long went in with him and the doors closed.

"I know you know Theodore Fry."

"I talked to him this morning. That doesn't mean I know him."

"I consider him a dangerous man."

"Just what the hell is all this? Will you tell me that?"

"Your sister's life is in danger. Yours, too, maybe."

"From Fry?"

Long didn't say.

David remained quiet when the elevator stopped and the doors opened. He headed out of the hospital, feeling angry and disgusted, and stopped halfway down the outside stairs. He faced Long.

"I'm going to have a lot of questions for you."

"I understand."

"You do realize that you've hurt my sister up there."

"On the contrary. I may have—"

"Don't say it. All right? Don't tell me that."

"I'll tell you what I can."

"Everything."

Long nodded. "Shall we?"

They continued down the stairs and headed into the east parking lot.

"David!"

It was Cheryl, running toward them. She reached them, panting, and saw David's expression. "What? David?" And in that little flutter of a moment, reading his mind: "Gin?"

"Something happened. They asked us to leave."

"Oh, God."

"She came out of it."

"She came out of it!"

But it wasn't good. He wasn't smiling. And this stranger—

"What's going on? Mr.—?"

"Long. My name's Matthew Long."

"He's a detective, Cheryl. Look, we have to go. I don't think they'll let you in."

And he was moving. Too quickly, too abruptly.

"David!"

But he was past her and heading into the parking lot, Long with him.

"I'll call you!"

"David!"

"I'll call!"

Driving home from the hospital, he watched his rearview mirror as much as he watched the road ahead of him. Long was there, following closely, Long the detective, trained observer, never letting David out of sight.

What did you say to my sister? What was that?

Part of a magical ceremony.

What was he supposed to believe?

What's going on? Mr.—?

He's a detective, Cheryl.

Was he?

Is he?

David pulled into the driveway and parked in front of the closed garage doors and got out. Long parked behind him as David walked onto the front porch, reached into the mailbox, and took out the mail.

When he opened the front door and went in, Long was right there with him.

"You're making me very nervous," David told him.

"I really don't mean to."

Long closed the door behind them. David glanced through the mail as he walked slowly into the living room.

"Care for some coffee? I'll make a pot."

"Yes, thanks, I'd like a cup."

David dropped the mail—bills, fliers—onto the living room desk. One long white envelope he held on to, showing it up to the light of the window.

Long was curious. "Something wrong?"

"No address and no stamp."

"No return address?"

"No address at all."

David tore the envelope open at one end and tapped it against his left hand, so that whatever was in it would slip loose. A small square of brown paper fluttered to the floor, faster than he could grab it.

It was odd paper, thick, almost like a piece of skin or hide or leather. On it, in ink or paint, had been drawn an odd symbol—a few angled lines decorated with circles.

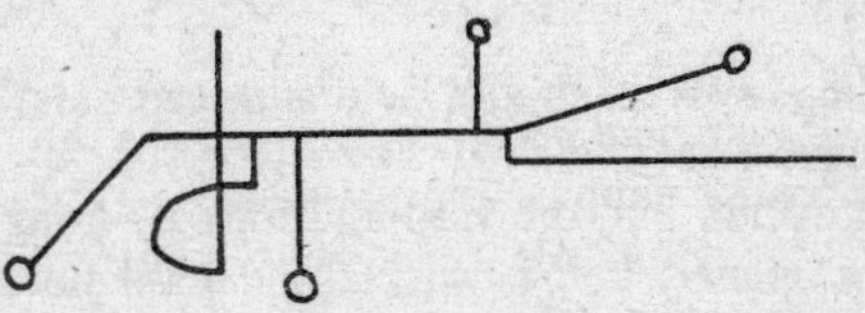

"That's weird."

But as David stooped to pick it up, Long jumped into the room.

"Don't touch it!"

"What?"

"Don't touch it. Get me something. Pliers. Scissors. Something to pick it up with."

"What're you—?"

"Just do it!"

That angry and disgusted feeling leaped inside of him again. "Okay . . ." He returned to the desk, opened the middle drawer, and took out his father's old ornamental letter opener.

He handed it to Long. "Here."

Without a word Long took it and knelt on the floor. He touched the brown square of paper with it as if expecting the paper to move on its own, like an injured bird's wing. Then he stabbed it through with the letter opener and stood, holding it out from him.

"You have a back door?"

"The kitchen."

David led the way through the living room into the kitchen. He opened the door for Long, who stepped out onto the patio and moved into the back yard. David realized that the grass hadn't been cut in a while.

David watched from the patio as Long took a position halfway between the back door and the flower garden. He placed the letter opener between his teeth, the brown piece of paper dangling in the wind mere inches from his face, and with his right hand reached into his coat pocket for a lighter.

Grunting, eyes catching David at the corners, he waved the lighter.

David trotted into the yard and took it. Long removed the letter opener, being especially careful not to let the paper brush his face or hand, and held it out at arm's length.

"Catch it on fire and get back. Fast."

David held the lighter under the paper and flicked it on. Fire instantly began to eat at the symbol.

Not normal fire.

Green fire. Green flames.

The green blossomed, sending up a pungent aroma, and the paper seethed, hissed as it burned and squirmed like a living piece of flesh, turning black on the end of the letter opener.

Squirmed.

Perhaps a breeze . . .

"Jesus," David swore, listening to it, looking at it move.

It didn't turn to ashes. It crumbled. Bits of it, black, dropping as flecks of dust to the ground, wafting to the ground.

"It's just . . . dust."

Long let it burn—crumble—until it was nearly gone. He flicked his wrist, loosening the last portion, which crumbled apart in the air.

Long stared at it until it was gone. He held his hand out for the lighter.

David gave it to him. "What the hell was that?"

"A weapon. If you touch it, he can find you."

David said in a shaky voice, "You're no goddamn police investigator. Who are you?"

In the kitchen he tried to make the promised pot of coffee, but he wound up standing there, empty coffeepot in one hand, the water running in the sink, the can of coffee on the counter.

Long showed him his ID. David took it, looked at it. He'd never seen a detective's gold badge before, but this, he supposed, was the real thing.

"So you really are a police officer."

"Was." Long took it back, slipped it into his shirt pocket. "I was a police officer. Retired—suspended leave—two and a half years ago. What I'm doing now . . . police officers aren't supposed to do."

''And what's that?''

Long didn't answer. It occurred to David that detectives turn in their badges when they retire. What was Long still doing with his? David had heard of rogue cops. Long?

''I suspect that there're some things of your sister's here that might help me. Letters. Books. Maybe she kept a diary. Did she? Jewelry or pictures or anything.''

''This Professor Fry—is he a criminal?''

''Yes.''

''Our police here already talked to him.''

''Listen to me,'' Long said. He approached David, not in a threatening way, but imposing. He spoke guardedly, making every word count, as if he'd never said this to anyone else in the world before. ''I've seen a lot of things in my life. I want you to keep an open mind.''

''Go ahead . . .''

''Theodore Fry is a sorcerer. He's a murderer. He's responsible for a number of deaths in upstate New York, and I've spent a lot of time tracking him down. Now he's here.''

''You're here to arrest him?''

''I'm here to do whatever's necessary.''

David thought a moment. ''Is that why you asked me if I'd heard of you?''

''I think Fry knows I'm here. But I'm not sure.''

''He wants to kill you?''

''As soon as he gets the chance.''

''That—square, that piece of paper or whatever it was. You said it was a weapon.''

''If you'd touched it—and you were supposed to—it would've completed a circuit. Manner of speaking.''

''And what would that do?''

''He killed my wife that way. House burned down in one night. I don't know if it came in the mail or if he handed it to her or what he did. But it killed her. I heard

her screaming. I couldn't get in to save her. I listened to
her die."

David was quiet for a long moment. "How do you know
it was one of those things, that piece of paper?"

"Fry told me." Long looked him in the eyes. "We're
playing a cat-and-mouse game, Professor Fry and me. It
ends here."

David stood there, empty coffeepot in one hand, water
still running in the sink.

"Convinced?"

David watched him.

"I know what I'm talking about. I don't pretend to understand it, but it's real."

David looked away. Stared at a corner of the kitchen.
Anything.

"Make us some coffee," Long suggested.

In the living room Long sat on the couch, still in his
trenchcoat, with Ginny's open diary on the coffee table
before him. The books, too—the books on magic and
witchcraft. And the jewelry.

He sipped from his cup, slowly turning the pages, Ginny's practiced, schoolgirlish handwriting suddenly becoming the weird cartoon cuneiforms which David couldn't
read.

David sat in his father's old easy chair opposite Long,
coffee in one hand, giving the detective quiet and time.

And finally, after practicing it in his mind several times,
waiting for the right moment to spring it—

He's a magician. He's a sorcerer, too.

—he just came out with it.

"You're a magician, too."

Long looked up at him. "No. No, I'm not." He sipped
some of his coffee. "I've learned a few tricks, that's all.
A woman in upstate New York. She was very helpful. She
didn't quite trust me, though." He was silent a moment.

"There's this whole underground out there. Mystical people . . . witches . . . this whole underground world of people. Like a religion nobody knows about. And innocent people get hurt."

"Is that how you lost your hand?" David asked.

Afternoon, and the sky outside was getting cloudy, the sunlight on the living room floor fading, darkening, gone.

"Or was it—?"

"Yes. That's how."

"I . . . don't know why I asked. Sorry. Just had a feeling."

Long kind of smiled, intrigued. He returned to the diary. "Not a lot here that I don't already know. It fits a pattern."

"That code. What does it really say? I asked Fry and he said it was trivial."

"It's about the things they did, quite frankly. Magic rituals. That sort of stuff. She was in love with him. Trying to reach your parents. Guilt. That's what triggered it. That's how he was able to use her."

"Why does he do this? Why does he do this to people?"

"I'm not a psychiatrist. I don't know why. I only know that he does it because he can do it."

"Is my sister going to die?"

"No, I don't think so. Not necessarily. But I think she's in great danger unless you take precautions."

"What happened? Do you know?"

"She opened a door," Long explained. "She did what magicians do—she opened a door. She did something wrong, and now she's literally caught between this world and the other one. Spirits are . . . dragging at her."

"What kind of spirits?"

"Spiritual forces. Magicians believe that life and death are the same thing. All of us—we're spirits in human skin. No heaven, no hell, no God. Just a big violent universe with different spiritual forces fighting back and forth. Like a war.''

David was disturbed by this. ''Is that what you believe?''

''I'm a cop.''

''But is that what you believe?''

Long told him, ''I've been forced to believe it.''

He got to his feet and picked up two pieces of jewelry from the coffee table.

''I want you to wear one of these. And I want you to give one to your sister. Tonight.''

David set aside his coffee, got out of the easy chair, and walked over to him. ''Amulets?''

''Talismans. They're called talismans. Maybe they'll help. And . . . pray. There are things out there—they may listen.''

David took the talismans.

''Thanks for the coffee.''

''What if I have to get hold of you?''

''You shouldn't have to, not after tonight.''

''But if something happens—''

''Route Fifteen Motel. Room 24. Okay?''

David nodded.

It was over. David wondered if he should offer Long his hand or say something. He still had coffee sitting there.

But Long crossed the living room and went into the foyer. David followed him. Long opened the door and told David, ''Thank you.''

''For what? I should be thanking you.''

''Maybe. Don't thank me too soon. Use those.'' He indicated the talismans.

David wanted to say something. He barely knew this man, he wasn't even sure he could trust him. He had more questions, but he hadn't had enough time to think about them, phrase them, sort them out, and the only person who could answer them had kept his coat on all afternoon and was going out the door.

Long said, "This isn't easy for me."

David looked him in the eyes. It was the closest thing to something human Long had said so far. Was it just his wife? Was it just knowing about the magic? Was it revenge? Two and a half years' worth, and many miles, the wife, the hand?

"Whatever it is," David told him, "what you're going to do, don't . . . Be careful. Shit. I'm telling a cop to be careful. I'm thinking of my sister."

Long smiled at him, genuinely. "I like you. I had a feeling I was going to like you."

Then he left. David watched him from the door, watched as Long got into his car and backed out. Not sure what he felt inside. Watched until Long's car, on the street, moved out of sight.

He closed the door and went into the living room, took an envelope from the desk, one of the bills that had come in the mail, and wrote on the back on it: "Route 15 Motel—Rm 24 Matthew Long."

He stood up and looked out the window, realized that his left hand was tightly clenched.

Sweating, tightly clenched around the talismans Long had given him.

And he realized that he was frightened.

Very frightened.

That evening in Ginny's room David sat and listened as his sister mumbled in her sleep. True sleep, he supposed.

He hoped.

He reached out carefully and touched her hair, just to make sure that she was really there and alive and that he was really there with her.

This whole underground world of people. Like a religion nobody knows about. And innocent people get hurt.

"It's all right, Gin. It's David." Whispering it, as if the harsh and sudden sound of his concern might somehow shatter her, cause her to explode like glass right there on the hospital bed.

What had he done by abandoning her, by refusing her?

He thought of that burning piece of paper or parchment or whatever it was, and he was afraid that Ginny would crumble into dust like the paper. David looked at her and realized that he'd walked across the street, he'd turned a corner, he'd awakened from a deep sleep to find himself awake in another world uncertain even of his own name.

"I'm just going to sit here for a while, okay, Gin?"

And she whispered to him in her sleep, maybe knowing he was there and maybe not, sensing him or dreaming him from wherever she was. "Don't let them hurt me . . . Mom? Dad? Don't . . . let them . . ."

"Oh, God, Gin, oh, God, I'm so sorry, I'm so sorry."

Far away, still, but a storm was coming in. Thunder boomed outside the Route Fifteen Motel.

Energy, collecting.

By the harsh light of the metal desk lamp Matthew Long composed a letter. He lodged a top corner of the motel stationery beneath the lampstand so that it wouldn't slide on the desk. When he'd finished he read it over, folded it in a practiced manner with one hand, and slipped it into an envelope.

He sealed the envelope and addressed it to Emma Daedalus in New York.

Thunder boomed again and Long glanced out the window. He'd cranked it open a little. Fresh air.

He stood up and pulled on his trenchcoat, swinging it wide to manage it with one hand. Then took his revolver out of his open suitcase on the bed and slipped it into a pocket. Dug his keys out of another pocket and put the letter between his teeth.

And left.

He pulled off the road about a mile from the motel to drop the letter into a mailbox, then continued driving out of town, heading east, the storm approaching quickly high above him, energy collecting, pulling him toward Theodore Fry.

I want you to wear one of these. And I want you to give one to your sister. Tonight.

In the bathroom David put one of the talismans around his neck. It felt heavy and awkward and cool, metal coin on a chain. He looked at it, turning it in the harsh fluorescent light. The symbols on it which he couldn't read.

He placed the other around Ginny's neck as she lay there, unaware of him, and moved it so that it sat neatly and properly in the little hollow at the base of her throat.

Cheryl came in, carrying a small shopping bag.

"How's she doing?"

"About the same. Asleep."

The room was dark; they listened to the thunder. David took the bag and turned on the lamp on Ginny's nightstand and moved the shade so that there was a little patch of light, a little oasis of light, in the quiet, austere, sad room.

"We're really going to have a storm," Cheryl said. "Hear it out there?"

The windows rattled a bit, a few feet from Ginny.

David emptied the shopping bag. Makeup. A *Cosmopolitan* magazine. A small unicorn doll, because Ginny liked unicorns.

"I brought her some stuff. You know."

David smiled.

Cheryl sat down and noticed the talisman, the necklace. She touched it and looked up at David. "One of hers?"

"Uh-huh."

"Do you think it's a good idea?"

David shrugged. Cheryl looked away. He went toward the open door and leaned there, looking out into the hall.

Cheryl turned around in the chair, following him with her eyes. "David? That man today. Who was he?"

"A detective."

"I know that. But what did he want?"

"There's been a pattern of crimes. He thinks Gin's is—"

Cheryl felt something on her hand, cool and quick.

She looked down.

Ginny's hand.

"Gin—"

"Cheryl? It's happening."

She was awake. The eyes bright, her hand closed strongly around Cheryl's wrist. Staring at her, whispering to her.

"*Ginny?*"

"It's happening. Take care of him, okay?"

"David! She's awake!"

"Cheryl, promise me! Take care of him! It's coming!"

David ran across the room. "Ginny!"

And already her hand had fallen from Cheryl's, already her head had sunk back into the pillow and her eyes fell closed and she seemed to be asleep again.

"She was awake! She was talking to me!"

"Ginny? *Ginny!*"

Long pulled up the driveway, going slowly, rolling up his window as the first drops of rain hit the windshield. He came to a stop in front and waited a moment, engine idling, not working up courage but just breathing it all in, not contemplating it but simply realizing it.

This was it, this was all there was to it, it was ended, it was over. The chase, the whole cat-and-mouse game.

He felt for the gun in his coat.

No more magic, no more bullshit. Just bullets.

He got out of the car, didn't slam the door.

Walked up onto the front porch.

Thunder exploded right above him, and a strong wind blew the rain down harder, in wavy curtains that swept across the lawn and exploded like a thousand little armies in the gravel driveway.

He didn't even put his hand on the front doorknob. Thought better of it. Something . . .

Instinct? Inner voice? Some sense of something. An impulse. Long was too seasoned to ignore it.

He came down from the front porch and looked up. No lights on in the house.

He walked around to the side, shoes leaving damp marks in the grass, and continued around until he came to the wide back porch.

A trick? Fry planting something in his mind, feeding him an idea or an image, Fry feeding him a sensation of paranoia?

Long tried the back doorknob. The door swung open.

Invitation.

The son of a bitch was waiting for him. End the game.

Why wouldn't he know Long was here, if he wanted to?

Pulling in a deep breath, he felt for his revolver and walked into Theodore Fry's house.

"Ginny? Gin! Wake up!"

"Should I get a nurse? God, she's burning up! Should I get a nurse? David?"

"Get a nurse, get a nurse! Ginny!"

The kitchen.

A spare room.

The dining room.

All dark.

He moved through them, revolver in his right hand, left arm lifted so that if he bumped into something—or if something bumped into him—at least he'd have a warning.

He walked very slowly. Literally pushing one foot out at a time, feeling his way with the toe of his shoe. A hole in the floor—something grabbing at his left—

Anything.

And even though his eyesight became accustomed to the obscure lightlessness of the house, Long proceeded as if he were a blind man, trapped inside something he didn't know the size of, trapped inside some living thing, listening for things whose identity he might never guess.

And the thunder, the storm. Above him, all around him. The thunder booming and exploding, rattling the house. Long knew what it meant. Energy. The storm being drawn down, the storm occurring because of the energy collecting here.

Because of Fry.

Because of his sorcery.

He reached the front foyer, the base of the stairs that led to the second floor landing and the upstairs. Which is where Fry was.

Long sensed it, knew it.

He put a careful, careful foot on the first step. Looked up. Kept his revolver out, head up.

Took the second step.

Thunder.

Wood creaked, a voice.

A light appeared at the top of the stairs.

Long almost pulled the trigger.

The light was a mist—a smoke or fog—swirling green and faint at first but growing, puffing, forming.

He didn't take his eyes off it, not for a heartbeat.

And from the smoke, a shape. A snout, wet and reptilian. Eyes bulging and eyelids flickering. Long black tongue snaking out, whipping back into the jaws. A lizard, but with human eyes. And huge. The size of a crocodile. Floating in the air, pulling itself out of or being pulled from the swirling mist, floating in the air.

Yet it seemed to walk, as if the air beneath its wrinkled paws were solid, as if the air were a carpet. It pulled itself along on the air, mist boiling behind it, eyes blinking quickly, head moving from side to side.

It crawled through the second floor banister as though the banister didn't exist.

And continued to walk, one flight up, over the floor, walking on the air in the dimness.

Until it disappeared, taking its green glow with it, more smoke whirling, above Long's head.

He watched until the last of the smoke vanished, blowing away, drifting.

Demonic. Something from the spirit world. Something from Fry's world.

Because this house was his world. This house, with its energy and power, Fry's energy and power. Energy, collecting. Tilting this house, and Long and Fry with it, into another dimension.

Long continued up the stairs.

"Get a nurse!" David yelled.

And thunder boomed, Ginny whimpered, the windows rattled.

And Cheryl, terrified, not knowing what— Cheryl turned and ran—

"Oh, God, oh, God!"

—ran from the room, into the hallway.

"Nurse! Somebody! Help us, help her!"

The second floor landing.

A number of doors led off it, and at the opposite end from Long was a final door. Attic door.

He felt the power coming from it and started walking down the landing toward it. As he did, another light appeared. Foam—green light—appearing in the darkness before the door like candlelight fading into view.

Long stopped.

Tall light, pulling itself, stretching, so that it seemed to rest on the floor of the landing. And as it took shape—

"God," Long whispered. "God, no."

A woman.

A nude woman taking form within the foaming green light, appearing almost real, standing on the floor, floating just above it.

"Carolyn!"

A beautiful woman, tall and slim. Black woman, nude, his wife, green-skinned, her hands behind her as if bound, head tilted to one side and the eyes closed fiercely tight, tears dripping down the cheeks as though she were in great pain and unable to communicate it.

"Carolyn!"

Long trembled, the revolver shaking in his hand.

Carolyn opened her eyes, bleeding tears.

"Kill him . . . Matt."

It was her voice, she was real, it was her voice.

"They're . . . eating me . . . The . . . pain—"

"Carolyn!"

"Kill . . . him . . ."

She began to disappear. Green mist. Back into the other world.

"The . . . pain . . ."

"Car-o-lynnn—!"

"Ite . . . ite in pace . . . Agla . . . Elohim—"

"Ginny!"

"—keep them . . . away . . ."

Thunder boomed so loudly, David nearly fell over.

Behind him, the door slammed closed, the hospital room door.

Trapping him inside with his sister.

More thunder—

"God! Keep them away!"

"Ginny!"

Long pushed open the attic door, revolver up, and the door opened like an eye, showing it all to him. The attic lit by candlelight. Dozens of candles, maybe hundreds. And Fry.

Fry with his back to him. Fry in a black robe standing behind a wooden table draped in red that was his altar. Crowded with candles and piled with bowls of smoking incense. Fry and the table in the center of a great black circle painted on the floor.

Magician.

"I remember you," Fry said, not turning around, hands up in devotion to his elements and demons. "I remember you. I suspected you'd come here for me. The hunger's been in you for a long time."

"It's over, you son of a bitch." He entered the attic but waited by the open door, ready with the revolver the moment Fry made a move.

"Your wife still comes to me. Did you know that? They all do. Whenever I wish. They're perfect, now, all of them. Carolyn comes to my bed and only I can comfort her. She loves me passionately, and she's in great pain."

Now he turned around, smiling, and crossed his arms upon his chest.

"That was her name, wasn't it? Carolyn?"

The smile—that smile. The look in the eyes. As if his eyes were holes revealing the other universe behind them, within them. Tunnels. And the candlelight and the smoke. The arrogance, the demonic arrogance.

Fry didn't even look at the revolver. Toy.

"You're in pain, too, Long. Aren't you? What have you seen? What air have you breathed? Where have you gone? And come back? You want to die, too, don't you? I know you do. The knowing. It's too much for you. The more you learned, the more you didn't want to know."

He felt that he wanted to cry—out of anger, out of hate. This was madness. In his rage and fear, remembering Carolyn, hating this man, this demon, this thing in the candlelight and in robes, he wanted to cry and pull the trigger, end it, end it, smash the life out of it, stop it from doing what it did, stop it from talking, from telling the truth.

Robes and candles, voice speaking, eyes seeing, commanding the elements, moving from one world to another and back again—

The truth.

"Knowing," Fry said, still smiling, but sadly now, patiently. "Knowing everything. You want to die now, too, don't you, Long? What have you seen? Where have you been?"

The tears came. His arm trembled and the revolver shivered in his hot hand.

Fry lifted his head, the smile going, the eyes darkening. He spread his arms out like an evil Christ, the robe falling open into wings, the candlelight around him an aura, a door of light.

"What are you, fool, to confront me?"

Long screamed.

Screamed, and stepped back, stepped away, as he fired his revolver—

Once.

Twice.

Again.

He was unbelievably frightened.

Things like this didn't happen.

Things like this don't happen—
First the window. Was it still a window? It wasn't a window.
She did what magicians do—she opened a door.
It was a door.
Lightning flashed. Lightning flashed and thunder exploded instantly, the storm on top of them, right here, right now. Lightning right outside the window, and the glow or flare or brightness of the lightning—
Held.
Just outside the window.
And turned green.
The same green, bright green, as the green flame of the burning parchment or skin or whatever it w—
The window exploded.
"No!"
Glass flying into the room, showering in slow motion over Ginny, shining like flecks of pure snow, shimmering, floating toward David so that he ducked, raising his arms.
"No-o-oho—!"
And as he ducked, green light burning, glass flying, he heard footsteps in the hall.
Cheryl. Nurses.
Now they were pounding on the door.
Pounding.
"David!"
The green light, vaporous, breathing or pulsing, came in through the window and filled the room, swirled around his sister—
"Jesus Ginny no-ooo—!"
Picked her up, the light.
Things like this don't—
She screamed.
God, she screamed.
As she was pulled off the bed, flipped over in midair as

if being raped by the green swirling light, like a cloud that filled the room—

"David! Open the door!"

Things like this don't—

The light was breathing.

Pulsing and shimmering around her, *breathing.*

And the wind. A tremendous wind trapped in the room, pushing David back, pushing him away from his sister, green wind, picking her up and flipping her over and over in midair, yanking the IV needle from her arm so that blood spurted, so that she screamed—*God no!*—screamed—

"*Jesus! Ginny!*"

"*David! Open the door!*"

He threw himself forward, fighting the wind, fighting for his life—

And the green wind, alive, the green light surrounded the bed and David threw himself against it and felt a surge of power crawl over him, a surge of power fill him and lift him, almost orgasmic, almost death, better than a car accident, better than almost drowning, the vitality—

He was thrown hard against the wall.

Pounding.

"*David! For God's sake, open the door!*"

He couldn't move. He shook his head. He tasted blood inside his mouth.

His sister was screaming as she floated above the bed, as she was yanked and pulled and stretched, as if the green wind were trying to suck her out the window or pull her toward the ceiling or smother her with more green light.

"*Leave her alone! Name of God, leave her alone!*"

He ran forward again.

And—again—the sound of a shock, the feel of a shock, the wildness filling him, the strength and the vision, the fullness and completeness for a terrible moment, a green radiance, the sensation that he wasn't a body, wasn't just a body—

And he was thrown powerfully to the floor.

"Da-vid! Open the door!"

Crouched on the floor, he reached inside his shirt and grabbed hold of the talisman, fingernails biting into his skin so that he was vaguely aware that he'd hurt himself, and got to his feet and came forward, holding the talisman out before him.

"Stop it! Leave her alone!"

—walk through the valley of the shadow I will fear no evil thy rod and thy staff—

It burned in his hand.

As soon as he came into contact with the green light, green mist that contained his screaming sister, it burned in his hand, the talisman, and he had to let go of it.

It flew, wriggling, almost alive, and shot through the green light and out the window, vanishing in the darkness.

God no no no no

"David!"

Pounding—

Sobbing, he ran across the room *get them in here* threw his hands to the doorknob *help me help* and yanked, pulled, screamed in agony as he tried to open the door and could not, the door that could be opened easily, the door that—

Pounding.

Cheryl and the nurses just outside, yelling.

The door wouldn't open.

"It won't open! It won't open!"

And Ginny screamed.

s c r e a m e d

And David turned to look—

s c r e a m e d

oh God oh God oh God oh God oh

His sister was being eaten alive.

David hurled himself across the room.

Things in the green light, demons, monsters *what are they* winged spiders *mythology* serpents with human heads, human eyes *hell* floating in the green mist, living in the green mist, pulling around Ginny, floating under her, floating beside her as she was pulled into the light.

Floating *through* her.

"Ginny!"

He tried to reach out, saw, fell forward, saw, screamed, knees hit the floor, *saw,* fell forward and automatically brought his elbows down, felt the shock of them as they hit the floor, *saw—*

As Long died in Theodore Fry's house, in Theodore Fry's candlelight.

The bullets had no effect.

Fry remained standing before him, burned holes in the robe, in his chest. Small visible seepage of blood.

Fry smiled.

The light of the candles dimmed, the candles sucking the brightness of the room into their flames, swallowing the light, pulling the shadows toward them, pulling down a veil of darkness.

As Fry smiled.

He crossed his arms at the wrists.

"Go to her."

And Long was thrown back, yanked off his feet. He slammed into the wall behind him, and his revolver clattered on the floor.

The faint light of the attic turned green.

Long screamed. He couldn't move from the wall. He heard noises behind him, noises inside the wall. The floor moved beneath his feet, the wood rippling like breathing animal hide.

He looked down.

There was no floor.

Long screamed again.

He was standing—hanging—floating over a black void, a deep pit, and far across the room, on the other side of the black pit, stood Fry.

Still smiling.

Long tried to force himself forward, but he was held against the wall and couldn't move.

And the sounds within the wall grew louder. Long craned his neck to look—

He shrieked like a madman as a tentacle, a snaky arm, erupted from the plaster and wrapped around him, held him, burning hot, holding him more strongly than a giant's arm.

Pieces of plaster and splinters of wood dropped below him, falling and floating like miniature lives in the endless void.

Long fought it. Fought the tentacle, fought to free himself. Shook his head to clear away the sweat and grunted, wrenched his shoulders, kicked, fought, fought.

He bent forward and, straining, saw something below him.

From the depths of the pit, from the darkness of space below his dangling feet, a reptilian face, an eel or a demonic shark, moved toward him, swimming up toward him. Eyes black pearls. Jaws opening. Stretching.

Huge. Huge maw. Empty. All teeth.

Long threw back his head and fought and jerked and pulled, twisted, tried to force one shoulder free, free one arm—

The jaws swallowed his feet, his legs, closed about his waist and tried to pull him down.

The wall behind him exploded again and another tentacle wrapped around his throat. It split into fingers and swarmed over his face, the fingers digging into his eyes and reaching, cold like gas, inside his face and moving beneath his skin, scraping his cheekbones, his teeth, pulling his face from his skull like damp paper—

As Fry watched.

Silent.

Long's body slumped forward and slammed to the floor, the neck snapping with a loud sound as it hit the wood.

The head bent. One eye looking out into the candlelit dimness. Eye full of horror.

What have you seen? Where have you gone?

They found him curled in a corner of the room, huddled, crying, sobbing like a lost child, his sister awkward on the bed, the nightstand knocked over and the window smashed and blood on the walls and sheets.

"Get security! Get Dr. Reeves! Hurry!"

"David! David!"

"Hurry!"

"Get Dr. Reeves!"

"David!"

In his dreams, in the darkness, he asked questions and felt nothing and someone answered him, Cheryl answered him.

is she dead is she dead is she

"Oh, God, David, she is, she's dead!"

my God she's dead she's

"David . . . David!"

the light . . . the window

"The storm, David!"

she's dead . . . they picked her up, they took her

"David, it was the storm!"

my sister's in hell and I can't my sister's in

"She's dead, David! Ginny is dead, God, God, I'm so sorry, David, I'm so sorry, but she's dead, she's gone, Ginny is dead!"

* * *

In the alone darkness of the middle of the night an old Ohio farmer with whiskey on his breath found him. Pulled his rusted Ford pickup off the road and stopped behind the car. Left the truck's engine running so he could leave the lights on.

He got out and walked over, in his mind images of other drunken men or a drunken woman, maybe some kids, but no killers or escaped convicts, no trouble.

Out-of-state plates. New York.

The car was awkward, half in the ditch, and the farmer tapped on the window and looked in. Squinted.

Colored man sitting there, head on the wheel.

He tapped again.

Tried the door and opened it.

Reached in, breathing whiskey breath, and with cool fingers touched the forehead, the neck.

"What do you say?" he asked the colored man. "Big one? Long way from home, my friend. Long way from home."

No pulse.

Big one.

When he woke up it was to brilliant light. Shapes took shape, shadows moved away, he was in his own room.

Breathing quickly. Horrified. Remembering. Still seeing.

my sister's in and I can't

Drenched in sweat, naked, he sat up in bed and breathed, gasping for air.

"David?"

Cheryl, in the doorway.

"David, are you okay?"

She came in and knelt beside the bed, searching his eyes.

"David, I brought you home. Don't you remember?"

Maybe he was looking at her, maybe he was just staring through her.

"They gave you a sedative. When you came out of it—you wanted to come home. You insisted. Oh, David, don't you remember?"

He felt his face crumple and he thought of a Halloween mask, a rubber mask stretched and twisted in all directions, that was his face, that was him. He fell back, moving strangely, and curled up in his bed, hid from Cheryl, sobbed, cried.

"David . . ." Panicky. "I just got off the phone with the nurse. I told her you were still asleep. Are you okay? David? Oh, God, I better call her back. David, do you want me to—"

A little before dawn Fry packed some necessities into a suitcase and carried it down to his car.

Then, before leaving, he walked into the woods that surrounded his home. The first sunlight was filling the forest; the ground was damp with dew and mist; small animals scurried away into the underbrush at the sound of the magician's munching, approaching footsteps.

He came to a small ravine that he knew all about and headed toward an area of boulders with which he was already familiar. Ancient trees topped the boulders, the roots knotting around them and under them and through them. Beneath the boulders was a small delve, a hole in the side of the ravine slope.

A weathered dog skeleton lay there.

Fry broke a branch from a tree and with a heavy pocket knife stripped it of leaves, twigs, and bark. He shaved one end into a point, then used the staff to draw a large circle around the dog skeleton, boulders, and trees.

As he did, he chanted.

"Levo hic spiritus neo mea inimici. Levo hic spiritus neco mea inimici . . ."

When the circle was completed, Fry set aside his staff and picked up handfuls of damp forest earth, dropped them over the skeleton, and continued to pile damp earth onto the bones until he had built a mound of mud.

"In nomine Bezemoth Ipsissimus levo hic spiritus. In nomine Bezemoth Ipsissimus levo hic spiritus . . ."

Then he went down to the shallow stream at the bottom of the ravine, pushed his hands in deep and pulled them out dripping, holding heart-sized balls of mud.

He sprinkled the mud over the earth-piled skeleton and splashed water upon it.

He pressed his dirty hands together before his chest, raised his pressed hands above his head, and spread out his arms.

"Quam oblationem tu, o Bezemoth Ipsissimus, in omnibus—"

Rising sunlight cut through the treetops and the mound of mud began to steam, raising a warm mist.

"—quaesumus, bene dictam, adscriptam—"

The mound of mud began to quiver, sinking into the dog skeleton.

"—ratam, rationablem, accetabliemque facere digneris."

The mud pressed itself around the skeleton so that a large dog of earth lay within Fry's circle.

"Veni, in nomine Bezemoth Ipsissimus."

The mud smoothed itself, grew black hair like grass growing quickly in a field. Dog eyes bulged beneath newly formed lids, damp nostrils quivered, white teeth showed, claws grew from the paws. Earth had become flesh; life had been raised, created, brought down, where there had been no life.

"In nomine Bezemoth."

The demonic dog shuddered. Moved a leg. Shook its head. Showed its teeth. Opened an eye.

The eye was red, demonically red.

* * *

Why?

Why?

He was standing in the back yard. Standing in a grave-yard. In his bathrobe.

Whatever happened inside her, inside her head, oh, God, it's not your fault, David, don't you see? Because she snapped or something and you were there, feeling guilty, God, and the storm, it closed the door, air pressure or something, but, David, it was like you were trapped there with her or something, don't you see? It would've been too much for anyone, it was too much for you.

Standing where he and Long had burned the square of paper. Paper or leather or whatever it was.

Why?

He wondered about Long but he was too weak to move, so he just stood there.

Cheryl watched him through the kitchen window, alone.

"Oh, David, David, what happened to *you*, what happened to *you*, David?"

In the shower he nearly fell asleep standing beneath the water, staring at the tile, staring at his wet hands, wanting to pull his eyes out.

And later, as he came awake slowly, feeling diseased, after he'd dried himself, gone through the motions, living somewhere else, he stood in the middle of his bedroom with his shirt half buttoned, hands frozen as they were caught moving toward his collar, and Cheryl came in, wanting to help, smiling sadly, and she started to finish buttoning his shirt.

He turned away from her, suddenly angry.

"Jesus Christ, Cheryl! I can button my own goddamn shirt!"

* * *

He had gone to seminary looking for answers, for solace, reasons, explanations. All the whys. For a feeling. Let me feel whole, let me feel complete, let me feel purposeful, let me feel not guilty.

After his parents had died.

Now he sat at the kitchen table and stared at the cup of coffee between his hands, and Cheryl, watching him, hovering, daring herself to do something, caring about him, wanting to scream—Cheryl was there and he could read her mind but he couldn't look up, couldn't look her in the eyes.

He couldn't move.

Couldn't move.

Cheryl decided to make him some lunch. Force him to eat.

Nervous, she almost cut herself. Good. Bleed all over the counter.

David was sitting on the couch in the living room, quiet, removed, picking at a loose thread on the arm of the couch.

He was watching television. "News at Noon." In a corner of the screen beside the black woman's head was a slide showing the silhouette of an automobile inside a yellow cartoon burst.

" . . . a one-car accident on County Line Road late last night in Stewart Township, which proved fatal—"

Cheryl came in, carrying a turkey sandwich on a plate.

"David? Eat something, please."

"—to the driver of the car, identified by police as Matthew D. Long, forty-three, of Hemley—"

"Jesus Christ!"

"—New York. Preliminary county coroner's investigation indicates a heart attack was the—"

"Oh, God!"

"David!"

He was up and moving instantly. Across the living room, heading for the door.

"David!"

She heard the closet door open and close, and he came back with his jacket on and grabbed the keys from the desk and turned again.

"David!"

He looked back, almost unable to stop because he was in motion, he was moving, he knew.

He *knew.*

"Cheryl . . ." Her eyes. But he said quietly, shaking his head, "God—" and ran out.

The insane thing was that he had no doubts whatsoever.

The insane thing was that he knew now exactly what had happened, what had happened to his sister and what had happened to Long.

He knew.

He wasn't sure what he could do about it but he was exploding and he had to—

Had to—

When he reached Fry's house he drove crazily up the driveway, sliding on the gravel as he braked to a stop. He jumped out, slamming his door furiously, and ran onto the front porch.

He rattled the doorknob. Locked. He pounded on the heavy door.

"Fry! Open the door! Let me in!"

Nothing.

Furious, he ran down the long porch and looked through a window, rapped on the glass so hard he thought he'd break it.

"You know who it is, goddamn it! Let me in! Open the door! Fry!"

He jumped the wall of the porch, kicked through the

flower garden, pulled out one of the bricks that bordered it. He stepped back into the yard, hefting the brick.

"Fry! *Fry!*"

Threw it.

It sailed high, hit the side of the house, and fell back into the lawn. David retrieved it and stepped back again.

"Damn it, Fry, goddamn you, you killed him and you killed my sister, *let me in!*"

Again, the brick.

It arced, smashed through a window on the second floor, and David jumped back, away from the falling glass.

"*Fry!*"

He wanted to kill. He wanted to—

He saw it out of the corner of his eye.

There. Across the lawn, on the other side of the driveway. Running fast.

A dog.

Large black dog.

Watchdog.

"Holy . . . shit . . ."

Loping. Moving—very fast. Very quickly. David had never seen a dog run that quickly, he'd never seen a dog that looked like this dog. The eyes.

He started running for his car and fumbled for his keys, his jacket flapping as he kicked up gravel. The dog wouldn't get him. It was too far away, even this dog couldn't move that—

He dropped his keys.

"Shit, shit, shit!"

Skidded on the gravel and fell onto one knee, still sore from his collapse at the hospital, got the keys, got back up.

Lurched for his car.

And the dog was close, now. Very close.

His knee hurt.

He gripped the door handle, yanked the door open and threw himself in, slammed the door.

Looked out the window—

"Shit, shit . . ."

Got the key into the ignition and turned the car over and gunned it without meaning to.

And the dog was at him.

It leaped onto the hood of the car and slid and scratched, trying to hold on. Sheer ferocity and momentum carried it off the hood and it landed on the gravel on all fours, turned instantly, showing David wide jaws, gleaming teeth, hellish eyes.

It jumped. Smashed into the side of the car, hit the door.

David felt the car rock.

Jesus Christ, this was no dog, this was no real dog.

He hit the accelerator. The rear tires spun and gravel exploded in a geyser behind him.

The dog ran alongside. David tried to steer the car to run it over or cripple it, but the dog jumped onto the hood again and butted its head against the windshield.

David yelled out loud inside the car and hit the brakes.

The dog slid off the hood.

He threw the car into reverse, frantically turned the wheel and shifted into forward, spun his tires again to escape.

And the dog was there.

Not on the hood this time, but slamming against the car when it jumped onto the trunk lid.

David saw it in his rearview mirror.

Clawing, barking, scratching, snarling, digging its claws into the metal, pushing its face against the glass.

"Jesus Christ, leave me alone!"

He accelerated.

The dog held on. Claws in the metal. David wasn't

watching the driveway, he was watching his mirror, and he saw—

A paw. One black paw sinking through his rear window, pushing through the glass but not breaking it, sliding through as if the glass weren't there.

David screamed.

The head, the mouth. Jaws, dripping, the nose and the eyes, all red, staring at him, seeing him, sinking into the glass, the head coming through the glass—

"Jesus!"

David turned his wheel right, left, turned it around, kept his accelerator floored. The car swerved and shifted and rocked, gravel exploded, he saw the mouth, the eyes, the paw—

And the dog slipped off.

David saw it go in his rearview mirror. He was on the lawn, the car jumping. He got back onto the driveway and continued so fast that he headed for the road without looking.

The rearview mirror. One last look.

The dog was in the middle of the driveway, staring after him, the eyes hot and the mouth dripping, not willing or not able to follow him.

Demon dog.

David braked suddenly at the end of the driveway and pulled onto the road, heart pounding, legs shaking, and drove away as fast as he could.

In agony, Cheryl made the phone call.

"Bob? Yes. It's Cheryl D'Angelo. Fine, thank you. Well, no, not so fine. No, not me, a friend of mine. Kind of. His sister died. Do you remember Ginny Trevisan? I think you met her once. Bob, she died last night, and I need— Bob, I'm okay. I am, I'm okay. It's her brother. David. God, Bob, I don't know, he's just, he's cracking up or something. It's hard, I'm very worried. He's not doing well with— That's right. David. Well, he did for a year but he quit and— Would you? Oh, Bob, thank you. No, I haven't said anything to him yet, he's just walking around here like— I will. Thank you. I will, Bob.''

The Route Fifteen Motel was a sad affair. It sat between a used car lot on one side and a deserted gas station on the other. The motel was L-shaped, and as David slowly drove past it he counted the numbers on the doors. Twenty-four.

He pulled into the gas station, a boarded-up concrete building with a cracked concrete lot with weeds growing through, and parked.

He opened his trunk and rummaged through the small cardboard box he had in there. Tools and a can of nails and antifreeze and oil. He dug out a small screwdriver with dried white paint on its blade.

A thin ditch filled with weeds and surrounded by stunted trees separated the gas station and the motel. David made his way across the ditch and, protected by the trees and the angle of the building, crept up to the window of room 24, five down from the end.

The window was not locked. It was ajar, and David was able to jostle it and swing it open. He used the screwdriver to pry beneath the frame of the screen window. It rattled, frightening him; he looked around constantly, paranoid, not a veteran of this sort of thing. But no one was around to notice.

He crawled through the window and dropped as lightly as he could to the floor.

Long's suitcase was open on the bed. David sorted through the contents, understanding that Long had obviously attempted what he'd promised to do: go to Fry's last night and then return here and then leave Noland, leave David and Ginny and leave everything behind. Job done, work finished.

Was he in torment now, as Ginny was?

Clothes. A Bible. Some books on black magic. A small case with toothbrush and soap and a razor.

And a zippered portfolio containing two decorative knives, boxes of incense, candles, talismans on chains. And an address book.

David opened the address book.

I've spent a lot of time tracking him down.

It was well used, with pages torn and taped, corners folded and unfolded. The blank pages in the back were covered with notes. And every name, address, and telephone number in it had been X'd out or crossed through.

Except one.

D. Emma Daedalus. Funny name. Her address was printed carefully in large block letters; her phone number was right there.

I've learned a few tricks, that's all. A woman in upstate New York. She was very helpful. She didn't quite trust me, though.

David slipped the address book into his back pocket and climbed out the window.

"I want to help," Cheryl said. "That's all I want."

She was sitting beside him on the couch, shoes off, legs curled up. She reached up and held his face, turned him so that David was looking at her.

"That's all I want."

"I know that."

"I'm so worried about you."

He looked deeply into her eyes, trying to signal her that he was all right, that he knew what was going on even if he couldn't say anything, that she could trust him, he could take care of himself.

"David, I know you think you know what happened. I know that. But I'm scared. You're scaring me."

"I don't mean to."

"Will you please just do this? For me? Will you? Just talk to him?"

"Do you think he can fix it?"

"I don't think anything needs to be fixed. I just think— Will you?"

He looked away, thinking of the address book, of Long. Fry. That . . . dog . . .

He agreed reluctantly. "All right . . ."

There was no victory for Cheryl in the sound of his voice.

"You're the stubbornest person I've ever known," she complained, getting off the couch and going into the kitchen.

It felt peculiar, sitting there in front of the desk, looking at him. A replay of him and Father Kendrick, just before— everything.

Father Mulhaney wore a shirt with rolled-up sleeves. No collar. A young man, perhaps as young or seeming to be as young as David. His office had plants in it and a small color TV and a VCR. On his desk was a sign that read: LIFE'S A BITCH AND THEN YOU DIE.

"Cheryl tells me you've had some bad news recently," Father Mulhaney said to David, concerned.

"That's true, Father Mulhaney."

"Bob. Just call me Bob, please. You were studying at St. Luke's, weren't you?"

"That's right."

"I understand you left. Not right for you?"

"No, I'm afraid not."

God, this was going to be interminable.

"Your sister died the other night, didn't she? A heart attack? You want to talk about that?"

"I don't know," David said. "I'm pretty upset."

"That's understandable."

"She practiced witchcraft."

"I beg your pardon?"

"I'm feeling very uncomfortable, Bob. Aren't you feeling a little uncomfortable?"

At the Noland City Cemetery the morning was overcast and it was drizzling.

In the tent on the hill a few persons were gathered around Ginny's casket. Only a few. Some of the people she'd worked with. Some of the neighbors who'd persisted in stopping by, making conversation with her for a few months, trying to adopt her after Mom and Dad had died.

They listened attentively, believing, subdued as people are when the cold breathes around their collars.

"—experience a merciful judgment and rejoice in everlasting happiness. Through Jesus Christ our Lord. Amen."

A few there crossed themselves. Cheryl certainly did.

David did not.

And afterward he walked down the hill and across the gravel drive to kneel beside his parents' headstones.

Cheryl watched him and crossed herself again.

For him.

They made love that night, David and Cheryl.

Made love out of friendship, the way friends will sometimes when intimacy is needed, understanding, trust. When words have been said and the words are a wall, when neither wants the wall.

Afterward David lay with his back to Cheryl, thinking she'd perhaps fallen asleep.

"What?" But she sensed something.

He realized that it was irritating him, her concern, her genuine concern. Because he *knew* and he couldn't talk about it except, maybe, with other people who might know.

"God, David, you've got to get a grip on this. Don't

you think I'm scared, too? We'll work it out. I want to stay with you. Don't you want to stay here? We can stay here and give it a chance. We never really gave it a chance. We need to lean on each other.''

He didn't say anything to her, just stared into the dark.

She was almost in tears; he heard it in her voice. It was as if he'd died quietly there beside her and she wanted to make sure he was still there. She pressed herself against his back and legs and wrapped an arm around him and laid her head against his shoulder. He felt the length of her, warm and damp, and her hair, trying to keep him alive.

''You're all I have. I don't have any friends. I love you. God, I love you, and I want to live again. I just want to start living again. You can't tell me you don't want that. We both want that. Don't we?''

Silence.

''David?''

God, she wanted to hit him, dig her nails into his skin, hurt him just to remind him—

''I just want to know what's going on!'' Cheryl said, hurt, sitting up, sneaking away from him. ''You're humiliating me! What's wrong with you?''

Now he rolled over.

Looked up at her.

Looked up at her.

''I don't know,'' he whispered, so quietly that she almost couldn't hear. ''But I have to find out something. I have to . . . find out something, Cheryl. If you think you can—please . . . trust me.''

He reached out to her.

She came to him.

Alone in the darkness he hugged her and held her, held her.

Cheryl couldn't take any more days off work so David was by himself the next day. No neighbors dropped by;

no one called. He wouldn't have wanted them to. Time enough by himself to think, watch the gray sky outside, make a pot of tea, and walk through the house.

Think.

Half dressed in his bathrobe, he sipped tea at the kitchen table and looked through his sister's diary, following her until her handwriting disappeared and he ran up against the impossibility of her medieval symbols, that Celestial Alphabet, posturing and maybe profound, reminding him of Fry and the dog and the hospital and all the evil David had ever been afraid of.

Because there was no way to find Fry now.

Was there?

He picked up Long's address book, read and reread Emma Daedalus's name and phone number and address. Phone number.

But he wasn't ready to commit himself yet.

He'd walked around a corner and found himself someplace else, but if he admitted that, even though he knew he believed it, he'd be there, he'd be there someplace else forever.

Without Cheryl.

He lost the morning sitting on the couch, feeling like a sick old man in his bathrobe, drinking tea, the drapes still drawn from last night, one light on, and he read through Ginny's books on magic and witchcraft and sorcery.

Magic. Ritual magic.

Black magic?

Well, ritual magic.

She did what magicians do—she opened a door. She did something wrong and now she's literally caught between this world and the other one. Spirits are . . . dragging at her.

What kind of spirits?

Spiritual forces. Magicians believe that life and death

are the same thing. . . . No heaven, no hell, no God. Just a big violent universe with different spiritual forces fighting back and forth. Like a war.

I think the universe is alive with many forces.

Spirits? Demons?

Names. Call them what you will. I have an enormous respect for the invisible things that surround us. I think human beings are just one kind of spirit.

All of us—we're spirits in human skin.

He read about Albertus Magnus and Paracelsus, Aleister Crowley and the Golden Dawn, the Egyptian Book of the Dead and Hermes Trismegistus.

He read about stones and herbs and plants, colors and candles and incenses.

He read the rituals. Invoking and banishing, commanding and cleansing, dangerously placing oneself at the center of a dark spiritual storm and dangerously wrestling with the wraiths and beings, incubi and succubi, angels and demons that watch us and follow us and keep silent until we call.

The magic circle of protection. The sword. The Guardian Spirits. The terrible names of power used by sorcerers to bend the will of the universe, to strain the clouds, to pull at the skin of the earth, so that nature itself will twist for a moment, following the magician's will.

The demons. The spirits. The celestial hierarchy. Whatever it is that is out there, called by human names. Dead spirits waiting to return, living spirits hungry to walk for a day and a night on earth, their old home.

A universe of matter and spirit that was not the universe David had been raised to believe in. Not an ordered, stable cosmos in which God watches over His people, designs moral purpose, forgives even the foulest if redemption is sought.

Not that kind of universe at all.

But a universe alive in its very essence, alive with the

meaning of aliveness, vibrant and pushing and pulling, swirling and chaotic, not knowing why it existed, a universe like some vast exploding soup containing many different kinds of life, spiritual life, and some of the lives at war, some of the lives eternal.

And at the center of it—

And the center of it, for sorcerers, for magicians, for mystics—

At the center of it—

Humanity. Alone but aware, frightened but knowing. Using ancient alphabets, ancient words, ancient rituals, protecting itself with spells and incantations, candles and jewelry—

Human beings using methods out of the Stone Age to combat and live with a violent, primitive, still-forming universe of life, spiritual life, angelic and demonic and hurting, aching life.

David had never considered the universe in that way, and it terrified him.

He had never thought of it as being *alive*.

An inert universe, put in motion by a God that people everywhere worshipped, by whatever name—that was reality.

But a violent, uncertain universe as alive as us, alive with infinite desires and forces and spirits and messages and meanings, a confused vastness that responded to calls and chants, commands and words, stones and colors and incense—

Was that possible?

Was that reality?

Was that—Fry?

Is that what you believe?

I'm a cop.

But is that what you believe?

I've been forced to believe it.

Is that how you lost your hand?
Yes. That's how.

He drove out to the cemetery that afternoon and sat by his sister's and his parents' graves. Not talking, not praying. Just thinking, and listening to himself deep inside.

Is that what you believe?

When he came home that afternoon he opened the drapes, started a pot of coffee, and considered that he ought to have something to eat.

Instead, he lay down on the couch in the living room and closed his eyes, trying to relax.

"David. I'm so cold."

He opened his eyes.

"I can't see you. David?"

He sat up, heart pumping wildly.

"Help me. Oh, David, help me. I can't see you."

Ginny's voice.

Trembling, he poured himself coffee.

Drank it, almost the whole cup, hot as it was, standing there by the counter. Drank it so fast that some of it dripped down his chin.

He poured himself another cup and looked at the kitchen clock, he didn't know why.

He heard something behind him and quickly turned.

The kitchen table. Ginny's diary was there. Her talismans. Long's address book.

He stared at the address book.

He hadn't left it open, had he?

Open, turned to Emma Daedalus's name and address?

Cheryl phoned him that evening after work. She wanted to come over, but David convinced her that she ought to stay home and get to bed early. He was going to do the same.

"I miss you. I want . . . I don't know, I'm lonely. I

guess I really miss Ginny and now I miss you. I guess I better not be silly about this.''

How could he tell her?

David did go to bed early, but he didn't sleep. He read, a cup of coffee on the stand beside him, his stomach knotted as he expected to hear Ginny's voice again.

Because it had been her voice. Either he was actually losing his mind—which is what Cheryl thought, of course—or he was under tremendous pressure that he wouldn't admit to himself, or—or he had heard his sister calling to him, even though she was dead.

He saw her in the hospital, in hell, in agony.

No good.

At ten-thirty he did something he hadn't done in years. He pulled on his shirt and pants and put on his jacket and drove four blocks to a 7-Eleven, where he bought a pack of Camels.

Then he came home, poured some whiskey into another cup of coffee and sat at the kitchen table and drank and smoked one and a half cigarettes.

They tasted awful.

The coffee tasted awful.

He thought of Cheryl and he wanted to make love to her again.

He almost called her.

But he was frightened for himself, because he might hear his sister's voice again, maybe coming over the phone.

David went upstairs, removed his clothes, took a warm shower, went into his bedroom, and turned on the radio.

At midnight he was packing clothes into a suitcase.

He slept for the rest of the night. Not a good sleep but the best he'd had in a while, now that he'd made a decision.

Knowing.

He awoke early and fixed himself a good breakfast.

Cheryl called from the real estate office a little after eight, and David lied to her, telling her that he couldn't get together for lunch or dinner because he was driving back to Cincinnati for a few days. Talk to a buddy of his there.

Cheryl was happy about that.

When he hung up he wrote her a short letter, put it in an envelope and, when he left, taped it to the front door.

Then he put his suitcase in the back seat, made sure he had his ATM card, and left.

Upstate New York ought to be beautiful in the autumn.

Part II

THEODORE FRY

The inn was deep in the forested mountains of central Pennsylvania. Once a grand old mansion of a locally prominent family, it had been renovated into an expensive hotel for wealthy guests, for businessmen on hunting trips, for lovers on honeymoons.

Fry pulled up to the entrance and a valet took his keys.

The lobby was impressive, decorated with stuffed animal heads and many plants, a fireplace that took up one wall and wildlife paintings and photographs of famous guests.

He approached the counter; it was marble and oak.

"Theodore Fry. I requested the ground floor, facing west."

The clerk, a young woman very polished and stiffly formal, consulted her record.

"Room 116. I think you'll find it satisfactory, Mr. Fry."

She lent him the register as the valet came in with his luggage. Fry picked up a small valise.

"I'd really prefer to take this one myself."

"All right, sir."

In his room he waited for the valet to pull back the drapes.

"Please let me know if you need anything else at all, sir."

Fry handed him a twenty.

"Thank you, sir."

And when the valet had left, he pulled the drapes closed again.

He dialed the phone on the nightstand and looked around as he waited. More hunting paintings. Plant life.

Someone answered, and he said ''Theodore Fry'' and waited again. ''Mr. Mabrey? Yes, I am. Yes. No, not at all. That would be fine. No, no, don't concern yourself.''

He hung up and walked to the desk, where there was a small glass ashtray. From his shirt pocket he removed a small phial. It contained powdered incense. Fry poured some of the incense into the ashtray, lit it with one of the matches from a pack lying beside the ashtray. The incense smoked into a thick, aromatic cloud.

Fry carried the ashtray to the window and set it on the sill, crossed his arms over his chest, then held his arms out and bowed once.

''In nomine Bezemoth Ipsissimus, ite, omnes spiritus malignos.''

He brought his hands together, pressed at the palms, and pointed his hands to the four corners of the room.

Protection.

Then he picked up the ashtray and crossed the room and placed it on the floor before the door.

''In nomine Bezemoth Ipsissimus, ite, omnes spiritus malignos.''

Again, he pressed his palms together and pointed his hands to the four corners of the room.

He had enemies.

By the middle of the afternoon David was well past Oswego and feeling hungry. So he pulled off the road to have some lunch and look at his map. He'd brought a thermos of coffee, a sandwich, and some fruit with him.

He was standing outside his car, enjoying the cool afternoon, the woods on this rural road, trying to figure out where he was, when he heard her for the second time.

"David? David? I can't see you."

His heart stopped. The knot coiled in his stomach.

In the woods. Fifty, seventy-five yards away from him. Ginny. Nude. Just visible, not completely there, as if she were a hazy image in a photograph.

Walking around. Not seeing him, just wandering, lost in the woods and unable to see anything, anyone.

"David? You're here, aren't you? Oh, it's so cold, it's so cold. I don't feel good, David."

"Gin—?"

But he stopped. She couldn't hear him.

Could she?

He dropped his sandwich on the road and started walking toward her.

And Ginny turned away, walking farther into the woods, still calling to him.

"David? I can't see you. You're here, aren't you?"

David stopped, closed his eyes, knotted his hands into fists. He pounded the sides of his legs with his fists. He tilted his head back and took in a deep breath, a long, slow, careful, deep breath.

When he opened his eyes again, Ginny was gone.

Sunlight. Trees. A mild breeze.

Gone.

Late in the afternoon he spotted a mailbox inside a long dirt driveway that curled back into the treed hills. The number fit. David turned up the driveway. He had to downshift, it was so steep.

The drive curled around and came to the back of a modest, two-story house of wood and stone. David parked and got out of his car.

Behind him, past a line of berry bushes, stretched a wide long field, brown and gray grass spreading to the horizon, to more trees. Ahead of him, behind the house, was woodland. And on the other side of the house was a lawn, neatly tended, giving way to grassy field. In that field, some distance from the house, was a stone barn.

It was charming, the whole effect; house and barn and woods and field.

David walked up onto the back porch. It was covered by a wooden roof and surrounded by trelliswork. He knocked on the back door, but there was no answer.

He looked around and knocked again.

A voice spoke behind him.

"Yes, sir?"

David turned. A middle-aged man, a big man with a full gray beard, stood there, dressed in overalls. He stripped dirty work gloves from his hands.

"Does an Emma Daedalus live here?"

"Yes, she lives here. And you are—?"

"David Trevisan. I'm from Ohio."

The workman came up onto the porch. "Is she expecting you?"

"No, I doubt it."

He offered his hand; David took it. This gentleman was as powerful as he looked.

"My name's Gray. I do the work around here."

"I see. Is Mrs. Daedalus here?"

"Well, yes, she is. She went for a walk. She likes her walks."

"Do you expect her back soon?"

Gray answered by looking off in the direction of the field beyond the line of berry bushes.

Out there, walking toward the house, was Emma Daedalus. Coming through the tall weeds and grass, wearing a light summer dress and a wide white hat. Middle-aged, David judged. Pretty. Like some Impressionist painting come to life.

She was carrying flowers in one hand.

* * *

They went into Emma's sitting room, a parlor filled with antiques. Old photos on the walls; old paintings. The sofa and chairs and the large round table in the middle of the room. A Victrola with books on top of it.

It should have been quaint, and it was, but David, pre-occupied, anxious, didn't see the charm of it.

He stood on one side of the table while Emma, across from him, arranged in a vase the flowers she'd picked. Not quite evading David but not quite meeting his eyes, either.

Gray stood in the open doorway that led into the kitchen. He said nothing. He watched. As if guarding entrance to or exit from the room.

"Matthew wrote to me," Emma said, moving the flowers. "I suppose . . . he's gone."

"He's dead." David was surprised at the edge he heard in his voice.

"What happened?" She turned to face him.

"Fry. Fry happened, Mrs. Daedalus."

She looked away hesitantly.

"And I don't know where Fry is, now."

"He moves."

"But I want to know."

"He travels. Like a disease." She met his eyes again. "Did Matthew tell you to come here?"

"Not exactly."

"Because he mentioned your name in his letter."

"Did he?"

"He said you're a priest."

"I'm not a priest. I was in a seminary for a while."

"I see."

"What else did Matt tell you in the letter?"

"He mentioned your sister."

"My sister's dead, too."

"I'm . . . very sorry."

"Look. I stole Matt's address book. Your name was in

it. He told me that a woman in upstate New York had helped him.''

''I see.''

''Trained him. In ritual magic.''

Emma watched him carefully, glanced toward Gray.

David leaned on the table for emphasis. ''You know what I'm up against. Am I wrong? It's Fry.''

''Yes . . .''

''I want to see him dead.''

''Do you?''

''Listen,'' David said. ''The first time I saw my sister in almost a year, she was comatose because the police found her in a field. She'd been there all night because of some kind of witchcraft ritual. Whatever she was trying to do, she did it because of Fry. So I went to Fry. And he tried to kill me. And I saw my sister die—horribly.''

''Nothing ever really dies, David.''

''Then I saw her soul, is what I saw. She's dead. And when I tried to get to Fry I was attacked by some kind of spirit dog. And Fry killed Long, I don't know how, but I know he did it. And I think my own life's in danger.''

''No doubt.''

''I just want to know what the hell is going on. I know what Theodore Fry is.''

''Do you?''

''And I don't think I have much choice in the matter.''

''I'm not a magician, David. I'm not a sorcerer.''

''Mrs. Daedalus, do you understand what I'm saying?''

''Yes. I do.''

''I don't have any choice.''

She could see that. At the end of his rope, maybe. Young man. Completely sincere. Everything Matt had indicated in his letter. Another—victim . . .

But maybe with the gift.

Maybe, this one, with the gift.

She looked at Gray. "You see? It comes back. It always comes back."

"What do you mean?" David asked her.

But she didn't answer him. She started to leave, going out by the door on the other side of the sitting room. She paused, waiting. She didn't turn around, but she said to David:

"You'll want to stay. You can't drive back to Ohio tonight, anyway. I have a spare room. It's rather cluttered. I'll make us some supper."

And with that, she left.

David, uncomfortable, uncertain, faced Gray.

Gray asked him, "Are you serious? Do you mean it?"

David didn't learn a great deal during supper. Small talk. Maybe that was best. Halfway through the meal he felt himself relaxing, his apprehension and anger fading. These two were people, after all. Emma had been married and her husband had died; that was when she had moved up here. She loved the mountains. Gray was an old friend, and they seemed inclined to be with each other. Emma bought the cabin, Gray worked to fix it up.

David told a little about himself. Not being circumspect, only careful. Would strangers care to hear all the details? But the kitchen was friendly and the home-cooked food good, and Gray made sure that two bottles of wine were emptied before they had finished their meal.

And when supper was done Gray offered to do the dishes, and Emma invited David outside to sit on the back porch steps.

The sun was down. The stars were just coming out, brilliant in the cool, early autumn sky. The moon was climbing and there were clouds.

"I'd always believed," Emma said, "that whatever is out there is basically good."

"I've always believed that, too."

"Maybe people aren't good but the purpose of everything—you know, nature, existence—the purpose of everything is basically good."

"You say it as if you don't believe that anymore," David told her.

"No. Not anymore."

"Emma, when I met Matt—when he told me what I'd gotten involved with—he described it as a war of spirits."

"It is."

"He said that the universe—everything in it—is one big soul. And the creatures in it, the spirits, are at war."

"The spiritual world is actually a dirty place, David. It's like this world. It's full of pain."

She looked at him.

"Tell me why you left the seminary."

He thought a moment before answering, wanting to be frank. "Because," he said slowly, quietly, "in the middle of the night, when I ask myself questions—I want to know what holds all this together. And I don't want other people's ideas. I want to find out for myself. Does that sound strange to you?"

"Not at all. You've put it very nicely."

"No one else seems to be concerned with it. Maybe philosophy teachers."

"Didn't you discuss it at the seminary?"

"Not as much as you might think. But I want to know. I'm the kind of person who wants to know."

"It's awareness, David. Awareness holds it all together."

"Awareness?"

"I want you to tell me what you know about ritual magic."

"Only what I've seen. What I've read."

"Does it frighten you?"

"Yes."

"Do you know what the difference is," Emma Daedalus asked him, "between belief and knowledge?"

He considered it for a moment, wondering what she might be getting at. "Knowledge," David told her, "is what we know. We know it. Facts. We know facts. Belief is—" It came to him. "We can't believe in facts; we know facts. We believe in things that we can't prove, that aren't facts. We believe in things that may not be true."

"Or may be true. What happened to your sister—do you believe that, or do you know it?"

"What're you driving at?"

"You've come to Gray and me, you're asking us to teach you magic. You're asking for something you know nothing about. You're asking to have your beliefs or your preconceived notions confirmed. Your beliefs are wrong. Your preconceived notions are wrong."

"You know that, do you?"

"Magic is an art of solitude, but you must never believe that you're ever completely alone. Because none of us is alone."

"Aren't we?"

"No. Never. Magic is what you went to the seminary for. It's what you do to get what you want. Magic is what other people call God. They think God is some kind of lucky rabbit's foot. Is that what you believe?"

"I don't know."

"Is it?"

"Maybe. I suppose."

"You know or you don't know."

David was becoming irritated. "All right," he told Emma. "Yes, that's what I believe."

"That somehow things work out? That God looks out for us? That basically the world is good?"

"Yes," he admitted. God a lucky rabbit's foot?

"Magic is knowledge. Magic is rebirth. Magic is turning awareness into direct action, and that, David, is a very profound thing indeed. When you work magic—listen to me—you're reborn. It happens all over again. When you work magic, you can hear God screaming.''

He didn't know what to say to that.

''Because,'' Emma told him, ''you're God. You'll scream.''

David stood up and walked out into the driveway, stood there a moment, and then looked back at her.

''All right. Tell me about Theodore Fry.''

''What do you want to know?''

''Everything. How you know him. You do know him?''

''Yes, I know him.''

''How?''

Emma let out a long breath. ''My husband and I. Frank was a businessman; we were both young. Fry was teaching college. They had some business dealings. In a way, they went into business together. At first it all seemed foolish because all we wanted was to be successful. But Frank and Ted talked and Frank was willing to try it, so we did what Ted told us.''

Ted. ''Magic, you mean.''

''Experiments. And Frank became very successful. And we watched Ted become this obsessed man. Because when you change things, David, you change. All of us changed. And Ted was hungry for everything. We used him and he used us. He became almost—evil. *Evil* spelled backward is *live.*''

''He said that?''

''Kind of a line of his.''

''Quite a comedian.''

''When people turn their backs on everything else''— she was playing nervously with her fingers—''when they have just one thing, when they're that self-absorbed— He wanted to try everything.''

''What did he do?''

''I honestly don't know. And I don't want to know. But

they kept it up for almost two years and then something happened between them, between him and Frank. Frank died.''

David stepped closer to her.

Emma said in a very low voice, reliving it, almost as if David weren't there, ''He woke up one night. He was crying. Nightmares. He was screaming. He became paralyzed. I didn't know what to do and I couldn't help him. He was crying like a baby and he couldn't move and all I could do was hold him, and he died like that.''

David watched her for a long moment. He asked, ''Because of you?''

Emma shot him a sudden, almost cold glance. ''No.''

''Were you in love with him? Ted?''

She smiled ambiguously. ''He's a hard man to say no to.''

No doubt. ''So you left.''

''I sold everything and moved here. Met Gray. Put it behind me.''

''Started a new life. Until Long showed up.'' He sat down beside her again. ''I need to know.''

''Yes,'' she told him. ''And every once in a while I hear something, I see something in the newspapers— I know what it is.''

''Are you afraid,'' David asked her, ''that he'll ever come back?''

''I know he will. He'll find me if he wants to. Maybe I deserve it.'' She faced him. ''He kills people, you know. Because he can. Just to do it. People hire him to kill their enemies. He likes it. He collects souls.''

David didn't find that hard to believe—to know—that Fry was some kind of vampire. He stood up again and walked back into the driveway, kicked some stones. Pulling away from Emma, being drawn back. This thing that had pulled him to her.

He looked up at the sky. He'd looked up at the sky ever since he was a kid. Everyone did. God was up there somewhere. Stars and angels and a throne. The perfect was up there, out there. Far away, just out of touch, until we died and things went back to being normal or things were somehow explained or just over, over and done with. Answers. And people so small.

"David?"

He turned around.

"When you do this . . . Some people—they can't stand it."

"Like Matt, you mean."

"When you draw the circle . . . when you light the candles . . . when you ask the spirits to come—they come."

Donald Mabrey was quite a young man. Younger than Fry might have suspected, and younger than he'd sounded on the phone.

He was sitting on the back patio, his wonderfully expensive home like a wall behind him, holding back the world, and a wide pool and long lawn and trees before him, his frontier.

There was a drink on the table before him, and when Fry was shown the patio by the maid, he found Mabrey simply sitting at the table, under the umbrella, sipping his drink. At his elbow lay two file folders and a thick brown envelope.

The maid excused herself and Mabrey stood. "Mr. Fry?"

"Yes." He was wearing sunglasses, although the afternoon was a little cool and the sun not at all bright.

"Have a seat, won't you? Care for a drink?" Mabrey indicated the pitcher before him.

"Thank you, no." Fry took the chair opposite him.

"I hope you don't mind my asking you here."

"Not at all."

"This may be a little out of the way, compared to what you're used to. Do you like the lodge?" Small talk.

Get to the point. "Yes, it's charming."

"You may not remember me, Mr. Fry, but we met briefly a few years ago."

"Oh?"

"At a business convention in New York."

"I see."

"I'm in a bit of difficulty and I understand from some anonymous sources that you're the man I should speak to about it."

"Go on."

"You keep a very low profile, Mr. Fry."

"Discretion, Mr. Mabrey. I find that, in this life, I'm simply a link in a chain. It's the way things come together. The people who need to find me, find me."

"I must say, it cost me quite a bit of money."

"Well, in a world sorely lacking in moral values, the only thing most people do value is money, isn't that true?"

"It is true," Mabrey agreed, taking it seriously and meaning to. He helped himself to the pitcher and motioned with it toward an empty glass. "Sure you wouldn't care for a drink?" When Fry waved his hand no, Mabrey set the pitcher down, sipped from his own glass, and said, "I'm not unused to difficulties. You can see by what I have that I'm an ambitious man. It takes a great deal of hard work. You can appreciate that."

"What's the nature of your problem, Mr. Mabrey?"

He leaned back. "I'm what you might call a financial wizard, Mr. Fry. But wizardry . . . it's as much luck or timing as anything else. Taking advantage of the right opportunity when it presents itself. Knowing it when you see it."

"Certainly it is." Fry nodded.

"The right opportunity, when it presented itself five years ago, was to marry for love. My wife's name is Elaine. You won't meet her today because we're separated."

"And she's your difficulty?"

"If we divorce," Mabrey confided to him, "I'm ruined. My fault, including her name in too many things. My lawyers at the time warned me. Now—I intend to marry a second time. For money. Yes, Elaine's my difficulty.''

''You do have a problem.''

''I understand that you can . . . manage things.''

''I can, yes.''

Mabrey stood up. He'd said it, he'd come out with it. It didn't bother Fry in the least, but Donald I'm-not-unused-to-difficulties Mabrey found it needful to take another long sip of what he'd poured from the pitcher.

''I've never done anything like this before. I'm a businessman. I can't have anyone know. Suspect.''

''Surely you've signed contracts where someone lost and you gained.''

''Of course.''

''Well, that's why I'm here,'' Fry said.

Mabrey set down his glass. ''I was told that your methods are unorthodox, but that there's no problem.''

''What else do you know about me?'' Fry asked.

Mabrey sensed something in his voice. He sat once more. ''Only your name. That, and a post office box.'' He thought it prudent, in the moment of silence that followed, to flip open the unsealed brown envelope to reveal its contents. ''Fifty thousand. Good faith. As down payment.''

Fry didn't even look at it. ''I need facts. The money's fine.''

''I'm trustworthy. I'd never—''

Fry smiled and waved a hand, interrupting him. ''I mean your wife.''

Mabrey reached for one of the file folders, withdrew an eight-by-ten color photograph. Elaine Mabrey was slim, blond, quite beautiful.

''Her picture.''

''She's stunning.''

Mabrey tapped the second file folder. ''I was told you'd require her birth date. And the time of her birth. Her address.''

Fry was scrutinizing the photograph. Finally he returned it to the file folder.

"She's expensive," Mabrey told him. "She socializes a great deal. I was told you can handle yourself in those circumstances."

Fry nodded.

"If you need more"—pointing to the money in the brown envelope—"give me a few hours' notice. And there's a list in there. Where she goes. Some of the people she sees."

Neither of them said anything for a moment. A slight breeze touched the fringes of the umbrella and Mabrey felt the chill. Autumn coming. Winter.

"How long?" he asked.

"Let me meet her. A few weeks—perhaps a month or two. My methods are . . . unorthodox. Sometimes, Mr. Mabrey, it depends on whether the moon is waxing or waning."

"I see." Not quite understanding.

Fry stood.

Mabrey did so as well. Quickly. He almost offered his hand—started to—but didn't.

Fry watched him.

"I look upon this purely as a business proposition," Mabrey told him. He seemed compelled to say it.

"As you should. Anything else? I'll phone from time to time."

"No. Just— No. Nothing else."

"What is it?"

Mabrey drew himself up. "Should I be afraid of you, Mr. Fry? Because I'm not. I'm not a man easily frightened."

Fry smiled. Odd smile. "Are you afraid of life? You don't seem to be. I'm just another one of those things that happens in the course of a lifetime, Mr. Mabrey. Like catching a cold. Like having an accident. That's me. Just another one of those things that happens."

* * *

Between them, Emma and Gray taught David ritual magic.

Emma told him why, and Gray showed him how.

They led him out into the back yard in the morning, and Emma explained that magicians praise the energy of the universe, the light of life, and that this was done by worshipping the sun.

"We pray three times to the sun. At dawn, at midday, at sunset. A prayer to life. And if you're ever not free to look at the sun, pray in your mind."

They prayed. In Latin because, Emma said, Latin was a noble tongue and the cadence talked to the heart.

"In nomine Sabaoth, Spiritus Magnus, suscipe me, o omnipotens aeterne, Spiritus, supra quae propitio ac sereno vultu respicere digneris . . ."

David told her that her Latin prayer to the sun was very reminiscent of the old Latin prayers of the church.

We borrow, she told him. Because somewhere at the core of every religion is magical awareness. "But this is older than any church. This is as old as humanity. The worship of the life force."

She introduced him to the special room she had in the basement of her house—a wide room whose walls were painted in bright primary colors, upon whose floor had been painted a wide double ring.

One corner of the room was taken up by a worktable, with its hand tools and paints that were used to create and reinforce the tools of magic—the sword and the knives and the brass bowls and wands. Candles were made here. The shelves above the worktable were filled with jars of oils and boxes of incense. There were bottles of colored inks and brushes and pens and paper. Even a small gas burner for metalwork.

David sat with Emma while she showed him how to crush incense into a bowl and how to recite the prayers used when lighting it.

"We're spirits in a material world," she told him. "To reach the spiritual, we need these things. Every scent has its own meaning. Its own association. And every color, every shape. Everything is connected, everything in the universe touches everything else, and you use the elements you need to get the response you need. Colors, words, incense, light. Look at these candles." There were boxes of them on the shelves above the worktable. "Everything in your ritual is planned in advance. When you become strong enough, your will can create what you need. You won't need the candles, you won't need incense, you won't even need the ring. But all of this is done to attract the elements you wish to invoke."

"Fishing lures," David commented, a little irreverently. "Bait for the trap."

"Only you're the one who could be trapped, if you're not careful. Look at the Tree."

On the wall behind him was painted the Tree of Life—the symbolic road, the series of pathways which the magician uses as bridges, a network of paths, to find his way when apart from his body.

"If you were walking on the highest bridge in the world," Emma explained to him, "and if that bridge were no wider than a ruler, and you were making your way across it—if the bridge were miles long and stretched between two mountains hidden by clouds, so that you couldn't see where you'd come from, couldn't see where you're going—and a wind is blowing, blowing hard, it can lift you off that bridge in a moment— That's what it's like when you're traveling the paths. Only it's not your body—it's your mind. It's your soul."

She pressed her hand on his forearm for emphasis.

"It isn't done by strength, although you must be strong, and it isn't done by willpower, although the will is the magician's shield. It's done by understanding that the path isn't really a path. The bridge isn't really a bridge. You haven't left someplace and you aren't going to someplace. You're already there. Everything in the universe is alive at the same moment."

"It's almost . . . passive."

"It's very active, but it's your active soul."

"When you light the candles," he repeated, "when you ask the spririts to come—"

"When you open the door," Emma reminded him, "you don't walk through the door. You will the door to pass around you. The door comes to you. The spirits come to you. The universe comes to you."

It was Emma who explained it to him, who introduced it to him; it was Gray who showed him.

In the back yard, when David was seated in the lotus position, eyes closed, it was Gray who walked around him like some Japanese sensei, intolerant of anything but perfection. Gray who pushed him in the small of his back to make him sit straight. Gray who roughly lifted up his chin. Gray who pressed down on his knees so hard that David thought his hipbones would crack.

It was Gray who told him that if he wasn't careful, he'd fall off the ruler-thin bridge.

"But there is no bridge," David reminded him.

So Gray pushed him again in the small of his back.

"Ouch! Gray!"

And it was to Gray whom David turned with the practical questions, as the first day and then the first few days with them passed.

"What if you attempt a ritual and nothing happens?"

"You did something wrong. Try again. You learned to ride a bicycle, didn't you?"

"And if you do something wrong?"

"Don't do anything wrong. Do it perfectly."

"But if you make a mistake?"

"They come at you."

"Across the barrier? Through the ring?"

"If you make a mistake."

"Is that what happened to my sister?"

"Probably."

"When I saw my sister . . . attacked . . . when I was at the hospital. There was a green light. I tried to get through it. It burned, it was like electricity—"

"Energy."

"Energy. When I came into contact with it, I felt—I felt strong, but I felt very calm, as if I could see clearly for the first time in my life."

"It's called an ecstatic experience," Gray told him. "If you'd known then what you're learning now, you could have banished them. Fought them."

"I tried."

"But you didn't know. You were here, you weren't with them. Your soul has to be with them."

"My sister's spirit— She's in danger, isn't she?"

"A lot of people have made a lot of mistakes, David. Don't you."

And it was Gray who repaired David's car. The ruined metal and the cracked windshield from the attack by Fry's dog. They talked about that, as well.

"Half here, half there," was Gray's opinion. "He probably conjured it out of bones or sticks."

"That can be done?"

"Anything can be done. You insist on thinking that everything you see is all there is. Tip of the iceberg."

"Do you know Fry?"

"Sort of."

"Am I right to feel about him the way I do?"

"Absolutely."

"Did you— Gray, have you ever killed anyone with ritual magic?"

With a look in his eyes: "Not yet."

And as they were walking back to the house late one autumn afternoon: "Is Gray your real name?"

"Why wouldn't it be?"

"Is it your first name or your last name?"

"It doesn't matter, does it? It's no one's business, is it, really?"

I just want to know what the hell is going on.

Are you serious? Do you mean it?

One evening after supper David sat with Emma on the back porch and said to her:

"I'm not sure I can do it. There's too much to learn. More than I ever thought. Too many things to balance. Train the body, train the mind."

"David, don't you think other people have come to me and asked me to teach them?"

"And what did you do? Turn them away?"

"Yes. I turned them away."

"And you didn't turn me away."

"You have the gift," Emma told him.

"The gift?"

"In your soul. It is your soul. You have— Maybe there are only a few people who have it at any one time. You have it. I sensed it; Gray senses it."

"Does Gray have it?"

"I think so; he doesn't. It's—ancient, an ancient gift."

"To become a magician."

"You are already. You were born to it. None of us knows why. Our parents only give us physical life; our spirits are much older. Ancient," she said again. "Magic works—magic is—because it's human. It's as old as we are."

David told her, "Once, when I was a boy, I was playing

on the sidewalk. An old man came up to me and said something to me. I didn't understand him. He took my chalk and drew a star. A star in a circle. I dreamed about it and I dreamed about him. Dreamed about ghosts. Animals. For a long time after. Scared me.''

''No dream.''

''Not a dream?''

''One of us. He saw it in you, too.''

David didn't say anything.

''You want to kill Ted Fry. You have the gift, you came to me, and I had to make a decision. Something deep in you, very deep, wants to kill Ted Fry. Restore a balance.''

''If you sense it, don't you think Fry did, too?''

''David, why do you think he tried to kill you?''

Hour after hour, day after day, long days and evenings into the night, Emma and Gray gave him no rest. Rituals to memorize. Names to learn and regurgitate. Colors. Paths. Alphabets. Formulas and invocations and evocations. Everything.

Everything that had once been known and now was known and protected by only a few. Philosophy from the Middle Ages and the nineteenth century. Books by Crowley and Levi, Regardie and Waite, Mathers and Conway. Ideas learned and lost and rediscovered, and relearned.

''The colors create vibrations. Energy. Yellow attracts the solar spirits; white, the lunar; scarlet, Mars. Names, only names, for the universe inside you. Invoke each time you light the candle and see the presence, see the color, smell it, the wave, the light.''

How many candles for Neptune?

How to reverse the lunar influence when the moon is waning?

In what direction to cut the pentagram when invoking the celestial spirit of Jupiter?

Can one circumvent the etheric Tattavic tides when they strengthen your enemy and place you at a disadvantage?

No one could learn it all, no one.

What human beings had learned from the Stone Age, knowledge and insight and behavior unchanged for thousands of years.

Ancient.

Magic.

Ritual magic.

Gray took him into the woods and showed him what branches to cut for which purpose, for wands. Birch. Oak. Maple. Evergreen. Poplar. Plants used. Animals.

"Because sometimes," Gray told him, "you'll have to take life, shed blood, offer the living blood of the earth to something so foul you won't be able to look at it. The day will come when you may need to do that."

And the names. Names of power. The nine hundred and ninety-nine names of the god-more-than-God—life itself.

Agla. Adonai. El. Elohim. Sabaoth. Agragon. Salus. Lux. Elion. Sadai. Otheos.

And the demons, the names given to the dark energy, to the unlight, to the elementals and the spiritual waste products of the universe, to the shadows.

Valefor. Beleth. Paimon. Buer. Sytry. Eligor. Mas. Morax. Ipos. Aszraoth. Kus. Belthal. Kothus.

Sigils. The lines and circles, the pictures created from the geometric shapes describing each spirit.

"The sigil," Gray said, "is the spirit's symbol. It's the door. When you carve it on a talisman, it offers guidance and protection. When you draw it in the air, the spirit comes."

David drew one for him at the basement worktable.

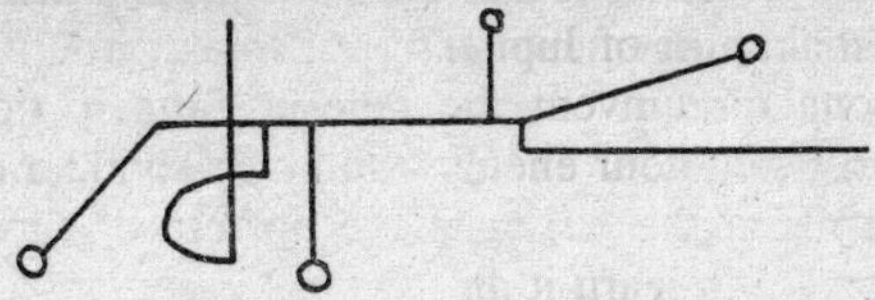

"Do you know what it is?" he asked.

"Yes." But Gray was upset by the sight of it.

"This is the sigil that was on the piece of paper Long burned when Fry tried to kill me."

"It's Fry's demon. Bezemoth. I don't even like to say its name."

Bezemoth.

David found no record of it in any of the books they'd given him to study.

They instructed David in the making and use of his grimoire—the magician's own handmade book of spells. Almost a diary, but more.

"It's the most important tool you'll have," Emma told him, as David showed her the first page of his, done on heavy art paper in colored ink, like some medieval illuminated manuscript. "It *is* you, because it contains all your prayers and rituals, everything you've grown through. Everything you are. You must guard this book. Protect it."

She made for him a white ceremonial robe and, dressed in it, David practiced his movements in the back yard with Gray. He held out a ceremonial decorated sword, the handle of it swathed in colored ribbons, the metal inscribed with symbols and words written in the Celestial Alphabet.

He traced his protective circle on the ground, lifted the sword to the four winds, the four directions, the elements, to call down his protective Guardian Spirits, to guide him and watch him as he prepared his ceremony.

"The light will surround you," Gray told him, "when you begin your ceremony. It's your shield. You'll see it as a blue curtain."

And late one afternoon Gray showed David how to cross his forearms at the wrists in the posture of supernatural defense.

"Ite in pace ad locus vestrum, o spiritus, in nomine Agla Elohim."

"Now turn your fists outward—roll them on your wrists—spread your fingers—show your enemy that you're protected."

David did so, holding his hands before his face, seeing the world through the web of his extended fingers.

"Should anything attack you, guard yourself with this gesture. Call up your shield. Speak your words of power. Banish them."

He had been with them for a month, and he had learned more in that month than he had in all his previous years of life.

The spiritual life David had desired, the truth he had sought—here it was, in his own hands, in his own mind, in his own heart all along.

I have to find out something. I have to . . . find out something . . .

You were born to it. None of us knows why. Our parents only give us physical life; our spirits are much older. Ancient.

Magic.

He had already studied her birth data and her horoscope so that he knew more about her than she did herself. Who she was and what she was, deep inside. And knowing this, Fry began following her. Shopped where she shopped, dined where she dined. Trailed her. Studied the way she walked, moved, talked, laughed with others. Deliberately bumped into her one evening, stranger to stranger, in the crowded lobby of a theater so that he could feel her, touch her skin, get the sensation of her.

And after a few weeks of this Fry followed Elaine Mabrey one night to a very nice restaurant outside of town. He took a small table by himself so that he could observe her from a distance, as he had been doing.

Elaine was dining alone.

Perhaps she was there to meet friends, but occasionally Fry had seen Elaine spend an evening by herself, reclusive, regal, beautiful, and poised, a lioness.

But he knew more about her than she did herself.

He called to a waiter and ordered a bottle of champagne delivered to her table.

Elaine was surprised.

"Compliments of the gentleman, Mrs. Mabrey."

"What gentleman, Paul?"

Paul turned to nod in Fry's direction, but Fry was there, standing beside him, smiling at Elaine.

"Fry. Theodore Fry."

Elaine regarded him languidly. "All right, Paul."

He left the bottle on the table.

Fry examined its label.

"Why the champagne?"

"An homage to beauty?"

"Cut the crap."

"Ah. An homage to wit, then."

Elaine grinned, looked across the room, looked back at him. "Who did you say you are?"

"Fry." He sat down beside her, helping himself. "Theodore Fry."

"Well, just who or what are you, Theodore Fry?"

"Oh, bon vivant, man of independent means, sorcerer, poet, anthropologist, thief, gambler."

"You forgot bullshit artist."

"Bullshit artist."

Elaine was amused. She enjoyed a man who was light

on his feet. She lured him with a look and reached for her wine and sipped. She passed him a blank cocktail napkin.

"Write me a poem, poet."

Fry crumpled the napkin and dropped it to the floor. "Mere words aren't enough to express the little I know about you."

"I think I could learn to like you."

"Care for champagne?"

"Not just yet."

"Made it myself from my own grapes."

Yes, she could learn to like him. A little.

Use him a little.

Men always came to her; she'd never had to go to them. What nonsense. It was never-ending amusement for her.

Elaine produced a cigarette from her purse and Fry was quick to light it with a gold cigarette lighter.

"Thank you." She nodded.

"Oh, it's far too early to thank me for anything."

Boys. All of them, boys, impressing little girls in the playground.

Fry lit one of his own and looked up as a group of men approached their table. Three of them. The foremost was moderately tall, well dressed, blond. Blond mustache. Born lady-killer.

Fry knew his life story the moment he set eyes on him.

He leaned on the table awkwardly. Been drinking. Ignored Fry and hovered above Elaine.

"Elaine! When did you get back into town?"

"Stuart. Just a few days ago."

His two companions hung behind, uncomfortable with the intrusion.

Stuart looked at Fry, eyeing him warily, not pleased. "Do I know you?"

"Are you sure you want to?"

Stuart sneered. "Collecting animals now, Elaine?"

"That'll do, Stuart." She wasn't in the mood for him right now. "Good night."

Stuart appeared wounded. "Now, Elaine."

His companions slapped him on the shoulders. "Come on, Stu."

But the drink came out. He shrugged them off, irritated. "Oh, fuck off! I want to talk to Elaine!" Leaning on the table, weaving in Fry's general direction, he announced, "I want to talk to Elaine. My friends'll buy you a drink at the bar."

"But what I want to drink is right here."

Stuart reddened.

"Good night, Stuart," Elaine told him again, insistence in her tone.

Fry stood, taller than Stuart by a few inches, not drunk, in control, just the first bit threatening.

The friends sensed it. Saw the light in the stranger's eyes.

"Yes," Fry said. "Good night, Stuart."

Stuart stood tall, removed his hands from the table.

"I can take care of myself, you know. I'm not that drunk."

But he was that drunk. His friends took his shoulders once more—"Pardon us"—and this time Stuart let them steer him away. He stood with them across the dining room, by the bar, looking devious and conniving, speaking low, staring at Fry with an angry, impotent, animal stare.

"I apologize," Elaine said, as Fry sat again. "He's an idiot."

"Well, at least your taste is improving."

She chuckled and reached for more wine.

Fry watched Stuart, reading the stare. Absently, as though unmindful of what he was doing, he took a pack of house matches and tore out one. He shredded the paper match stem as he and Elaine talked. Four thin strips pulled up the sides—two arms, two short legs, the tip a head.

"I haven't seen you in here before," Elaine commented.

"I just got into town today."

"Do you travel?"

"Yes."

"What're you doing here? Know anyone?"

"Actually, I know your husband."

Her attitude changed. "Do you? He never mentioned you."

Stuart was still watching him; he reached inside his jacket for a cigarette.

Fry laid his paper match figurine in a glass ashtray, struck a second match and lit the feet.

"I just met him today, too," he told Elaine. "Has to do with the divorce proceedings?"

Stuart lifted a cigarette to his lips, flicked his lighter. It sparked. No flame.

"There aren't going to be any divorce proceedings, Mr. Fry."

"Funny. Your husband said the same thing."

The match legs blackened and curled. The arms caught fire.

"What is that?" Elaine asked. "What're you doing there?"

The match head burst into flames.

And Stuart's plastic lighter clicked—sparked—lit—

Exploded.

He screamed.

The flame blew up in his face. His mustache cindered; a ball of bright orange captured his face. Little knots of fire danced in his hair. In the same moment, his hand disappeared in a loud burst of red, and a sheet of blood seemed to hang in the air before him. Slowly it fanned out, painting the men beside him.

Arms reached out as his friends pulled at him.

Elaine turned, staring in shock.

Stuart fell forward, sinking to his knees and twisting to one side.

One of his friends fell on top of him, awkwardly trying to suffocate the fire. He grabbed Stuart's head. The other went for the end of his arm; blood was shooting into the air.

A woman at one of the other tables shrieked and pointed, and the entire restaurant turned toward the bar. Some people stood up.

Stuart's screams filled the room.

A waiter ran over, and the maitre d'.

One of the barmaids reached for a wall phone and frantically dropped it.

The waiter tore off his jacket and threw it around Stuart's head and grabbed him by the neck. His pants became soaked with the blood pouring onto the carpet.

Elaine faced Fry, who was watching the whole thing dispassionately.

Her face had gone completely white. She looked at the cinders in the ashtray. Then she looked at Fry again. Her voice was thick, very heavy.

"Who are you?"

Evening.

From his window in the spare room on the second floor of Emma's house, David looked out at the dying day, the trees silhouetted against the purple, the leaves fallen upon the grass, brown grass.

There was a light knock on his door.

Emma entered.

He told her, "I think I can taste the first bit of winter in the air."

"Yes."

"I've been thinking. The girl I told you about? Cheryl? I've been thinking about her."

"Gray and I have devised a test for you, David."

"A test?"

The stone house.

In the cool evening, in the drizzle against which Emma and Gray had put on heavy jackets, the stone house seemed monolithic, the great black single door on it an animal's hunting eye in the mist.

The three of them crossed the damp grass, their shoes and boots sucking at the lawn.

"It was a storage barn," Emma told David. "Gray and I consecrated it for protection. When we place you in there, you must tell us what you experience and how you re-acted."

"And that's how I pass the test?"

"Yes," Gray said.

"Did Long pass?"

"You want to think about yourself, now."

Is that how you lost your hand?

Yes. That's how.

Gray pulled the door open. It hadn't been opened in a long time; good thing Gray was a big man. David stepped inside.

It had no windows; they'd been bricked up. The barn appeared to be completely vacant. David walked into it cautiously. The floor was nothing but hard-packed earth.

He stood in the middle of the stone house and looked back at Gray and Emma, two shadows in the frame of the doorway.

"If you decide to leave before we come for you," Emma told him, "stay just outside the door. Don't try to cross the lawn."

She spoke, but he couldn't see her face, not her eyes, not her mouth.

Gray told him, "There's a barrier around this place. Don't cross it."

David waited in the dimness as they backed out and closed the heavy door, heavy sound, so that he was alone in the darkness.

Is that how you lost your hand?

He heard something fall across the door.

A lock? A bar?

Stand just outside the door?

A test—or a trap?

He reminded himself that he had lived with these people for a month, they had taught him, they had trained him, and they wouldn't jeopardize his safety because too much was at stake; he trusted them—

Trust didn't matter.

He had himself.

Himself, and the ruler-thin bridge in the mist.

That was it.

You must tell us what you experience and how you re-acted.

Silent. So silent. Very silent.

Not even the sound of the rain, the drizzling rain.

Not even the sound of his own heart, the blood in his ears.

Where was he?

David took in a deep breath to calm himself.

Why should he not be calm?

So silent . . .

He heard the sound of wind.

But he didn't feel the wind.

He saw a light, a small dot of light in the darkness.

But he heard nothing, and he felt no wind.

The light enlarged.

It became green.

Just as the light had been green in the hospital room, in Ginny's room, his dying sister's room—

The wind made sounds.

And in the growing green light a shape appeared. Smoky. Very small.

It grew.

David watched it and as he did, he began to sweat.

The bridge, the bridge . . .

He closed his eyes, opened them, studied the light, the shape.

Still growing. Growing in the green light and smoke, although David smelled no smoke—

Oh, God.

Eyes. Jaws? Teeth . . .

Demonic.

The light exploded, exploded in his eyes, white and green light, smoke, and the demon grew, the demon exploded, the demon came at him, came at him—

Ginny—

Came at him.

David dropped to his knees and lifted his arms, crossed his arms at the wrists and forced his head back to look, to see—

—to stare at the demon, look it in the eyes.

When they opened the door they were no longer silhouettes standing against the darkness, but voices in the darkness itself.

"David?"

He was standing in the center of the stone house, staring at them.

Staring at them.

"David . . . ?"

"I saw—things."

Gray waited a moment. "What kind of 'things'?"

"An army of them. Surrounded me. Filled the room. Came at me." His voice didn't seem strange; he seemed—

"Watched me. All night long. I saw them . . . but I didn't feel them."

He took a step forward.

"I didn't feel them," David said. "They weren't real. Emma. Gray. It was a trick, wasn't it?"

"Oh, David!"

She hurried to him and embraced him.

"A trick," he said, looking over her shoulder at Gray.

Gray nodded. "Movies. Mirrors. Screens. All along the walls."

"And I had to be able to tell."

"You can't trust your senses, David. You have to see with your heart. You have to see with your instincts. With your soul."

With your soul.

Alone, inaccurate, egoistic, a mask in a world of faces, Elaine was not what she seemed. She ached, she hurt, but not romantically. She would have been dismissed as disillusioned, had she any illusions. But the events of her life, all of them, had been ill-timed. Mistakes seemed to happen to her without invitation, and she considered them profound messages. The purpose for her being on earth seemed like a hall of mirrors to her, mirrors reflecting what she knew about herself. She was vain. She was untrustworthy. She was shallow. She was a fool.

And she was enthralled by Theodore Fry. Not afraid of him.

He was a sorcerer.

The anachronism of it, the unmodern enormity and darkness and grotesqueness of it, the extreme isolation and melancholy of it, did not impress her. She did not realize those things. Elaine's world was quite small.

But he was someone stronger than herself.

He spoke in a language that was foreign to her but which seemed perfect.

No matter what he was, he was remarkable.

And Elaine enjoyed remarkable men.

But now, with Fry, all the money men and the power men and the businessmen became for her dullards, merely unimaginative, trapped by the earth and their own limitations, possessed by the very things they wished to possess.

But not Fry. Fry wasn't a man; he was a force, a presence. He was remarkable.

When they made love—made love the very night Stuart had fallen and died, burning horribly—Elaine was enchanted by his surprises as Fry plundered her. He re-created her there in her home, in her own bed, her passions coming alive like living things within her.

She saw things when Fry made love to her, and it frightened Elaine, but it made Fry perfect.

To set men on fire and to read her mind, read her body, all of her, to know her unquestionably—

Sorcerer.

He was perfect.

Afterward, panting, wet, relaxed, intoxicated, she asked him as he lay beside her, "He hired you to kill me?"

"Yes."

Elaine laughed outrageously. "He loves me terribly."

"Does he?"

"Oh, yes. To want to kill me? Oh, yes."

"I can still kill you, you know."

"Do you want to?" And when he didn't answer: "Let's kill him instead."

"He's paying me an awful lot of money."

"Is it the money?"

"No."

Moving closer to him: "What is it, then?"

He breathed on her hair, licked her eyelashes, breathed into her mouth. "Life," he said.

"That's it? Life?"

"You've never not been alive, have you?" Fry told her.

In the evening, just before dusk, he stood on the edge of the bluff and looked down into a valley. The tops of the trees far below were touched with orange, dying fire from the dying sun. Dying day.

He was dressed in the white robe Emma had made for him, and Emma and Gray were there with him.

The evening was cool. Fallen leaves moved along the ground, brushed by the wind, clacking like large insects as they rolled.

Gray set down a long satchel.

Emma said to David, "You must begin your invocation with the last light of day."

"I understand."

"You should have brought your grimoire," Gray told him.

"I've memorized the ritual."

"That's dangerous."

David shrugged.

Emma put her hands on his shoulders. "Look at me, David." He turned his face. Half shadow, half light. "This is the holiest thing a magician can do. The initiation. If you're not prepared—"

"I'm ready. I want this."

She kissed him briefly on the cheek. "You have a great gift, David. You'll be welcomed."

She stepped back and stood beside Gray, looking at David as if it were the last time. Gray bowed his head tersely. "Dominus vobiscum, adeptus."

David nodded. "Magister. Magistra."

They left him, went back down the path and into the

woods, heading through the trees for the house a mile away, where they would stay up all night.

David sat down and stared at the sun, opened the satchel Gray had brought.

A sword. A brass bowl. Incense. Matches.

The Bornless Ritual of self-initiation. To reduce oneself to nothing, to pure spirit. To leave this plane and journey the paths to the next world, to enter the universe naked, armed only with one's own soul, courage, honesty. To face the forever. And to return reborn, enlightened, a spirit in flesh, with the knowledge of All That Is.

Godhood, to the ancients.

Wisdom.

Empowered with the power of sorcery, of magic, in a world of flesh and stone, a world of roots and winds, brick and steel. To be awake while others sleep. To be certain while others doubt.

To walk the world with a divine secret.

To die almost, to slay the old self and become resurrected, whole, new.

The last edge of the sun slipped behind the far trees.

David stood up. Sucked in a breath. Pressed his palms together before his chest, raised them above his forehead, made fists, crossed his forearms. Spread out his arms, hands open.

"In nomine Sabaoth Elohim."

He bowed his head.

"Elion."

He crossed his arms over his chest.

"Amathia."

He spread his arms again.

"On."

He knelt and took up the sword.

Is that how you lost your hand?

He aimed it out from his waist so that the point touched the ground.

Yes. That's how.

He turned slowly—"In nomine Sabaoth Elohim"—as he described around him a circle on the ground.

Then he lifted the sword so that it pointed upward. He tilted his head, faced the tall dark evening sky, the clouds of it all moonlit, the stars very far away but inside him.

"Dirigatur, o Agla Elohim, oratio mea, sicut incensum, in conspectu tuo. Elevatio manuum mearum sacrificium vespertinum."

Is that what happened to my sister?

Probably.

He lowered the sword and faced east and cut a five-pointed star in the air.

"Veni, Oriensis, defende me!"

He faced south, cut the star.

"Veni, Astralis, defende me!"

He faced west.

"Veni, Gabrilis, defende me!"

North.

"Veni, Urielis, defendere me!"

He set down the sword and stooped to the brass bowl, poured powdered incense into it, and lit the incense with a wooden match. Smoke lifted, aromatic.

David stood up again.

"By Imanel and by Arnamon! By Memeon and Existon! By Agla and Amator! By Emites and Enitor!"

You have the gift. In your soul.

He pressed his palms together before his chest, raised them to his forehead, lifted out his arms.

This is the holiest thing a magician can do.

"Bornless One! Spiritus! I call upon You, Maker of Earth and the Heavens! Creator of Night and Day! Creator of Shadow and Light! Osoronophris! Iabas! Iapas! Voice of All Things! I am here! I am Your Voice!"

He bowed his head, lifted it back.

A wind answered him.

Slow wind becoming a strong wind.

"Bornless One!"

His robe whipped around his legs, pressed against his chest.

"Spiritus! Osoronophris! Iabas! Iapas!"

How have we failed you?

"I am here! I am Your Voice!"

Magic is what other people call God.

"I am the Bornless Spirit!"

Stronger wind, blowing against his hair, chilling him. He was sweating, and the wind was cool.

"I am the Bornless Spirit! I am the Voice! Imanel! Arnamon! I am Osoronophris! I am Iabas! I am Iapas! I am the Truth! I am the Earth and the Heavens! I am the Night and the Day! I am the Shadow and the Light! I am the Voice of All things! I am Born and I am Bornless!"

To reduce oneself to nothing, to pure spirit.

To face the forever.

The wind grew stronger. Around him, tall trees began to creak. The sun itself was gone, as though forced away by the might of the wind, the storm. Leaves and dust, branches pulled into the air around David and scattered away from him.

"Come before me! I am You! Make all Spirits subject to me! I am all Spirits! Earth and Fire! Air and Water! I am Bornless! Aeior!"

Godhood, to the ancients.

"I am revealed unto myself! I am All That Is! All is revealed before me! I speak in all tongues! I see with all eyes! I hear with all sensations! I am All! I am All and I am One! Aeior!"

Wisdom.

"Aeior!"

Wisdom . . .

"Aeior!"

Magic.

Did the wind explode? The sun die? The earth rise and fall?

David coughed, screamed more, coughed, slumped to the ground.

Godhood, to the ancients . . .

Still the wind blew, the wind he had invoked, called up out of himself, his own soul of storms. He gulped air. Trees groaned and swayed behind him, all around him, and dust and leaves and parts of the earth, in revolt, un-used to this, blew around him and blew away.

David pulled himself into the lotus position, leaned back and tilted his head, closed his eyes, opened his eyes.

I am—

The world tilted.

Air moved.

Thunder cracked.

For him.

"I am," he whispered, beginning to feel that he was suffocating, exhausted, "Bornless. I am Unborn. All That Is, I am. I am the All and the One! Light! Shadow . . . Osoronophris . . . Aeior . . ."

The wind—

Bornless.

The world tilted, darkened, began to disappear.

David began to disappear.

Around him, following the circle he had inscribed in the earth, blue light glowed and spread upward delicately. Rose like a wall, a hollow column, a curtain. Lifted to-ward the stars.

Protecting him.

The darkness melts away, or David opens his eyes, and he is standing, naked, standing in new darkness.

He looks down.

He is floating in the darkness.

He can still hear the thunder far away, and now he can

feel the rain, just drizzling, striking him, cooling his hot body.

"Charles? See? Look at him."

It is his mother's voice.

David turns—

Far off in the distance is a white light.

Two white lights.

They approach him.

His mother and father. But they're not looking at him. Something below them—and now David sees it.

Himself, a baby, in a crib.

His father smiles.

David wants to call out to them.

Abruptly their expressions change. Their faces change and the crib fades away, into the blackness. Mother and Father open their mouths to scream, they scream slightly, and blood erupts from their faces, their faces shatter like glass.

"No! No-oho!"

The car accident.

"Don't let them die! I can't let them die!"

And the wind comes again. The pieces of faces, like glass, blow away and David feels himself being blown away as well, pulled away, and he's alone in the darkness.

It's your mind. It's your soul . . . You haven't left someplace and you aren't going to someplace. You're already there.

"David? They're dead, David."

Ginny.

She floats out of the darkness, materializing, a young girl. Young Ginny. Ten or eleven, but dressed like a baby and standing facing him, holding a jump rope.

The ends of the jump rope, the handles, are lighted candles.

"Ginny . . . ?"

"Why didn't you save them, David?"

Tears run down his face. "Gin? *Ginny!*"

Ginny changes. A white light begins to glow around her and the wind sweeps around her, her clothes are torn off, the candles vanish, Ginny stands naked before him and she is glowing, her body is glowing.

She's looking at David but she doesn't seem to see him. "Oh, David, where are you? I can't see you! David?" *"Ginny!"*

But she vanishes. Pulled away quickly into the darkness, the eternal darkness.

David floats.

Behind him he sees a silver cord stretching far away. He feels confused but relieved, he feels alive. He sees more white light. Three white lights. Coming toward him.

Three white faces.

Robes.

White faces like porcelain and robes like gossamer.

They're watching him, and one of them moves ahead and lifts an arm.

David follows the gesture.

Far off in the distance, away from them, there appears a huge mountain, rising out of the darkness. Below it and above it, around it, are whirling stars.

Not stars. People. Miniscule people, tiny lights writhing, floating before the face of the mountain. Whirlpools of them, waves of them.

The foremost of the Three says to David: "Souls. Waiting to return."

David stares at the white porcelain face.

"Life is all," the Being tells him. "There is nothing that is not life."

It approaches David. Approaches but does not approach. David senses that the Being will come near and instantly it is there before him.

David feels immeasurable calm, he feels the profound

strength, the power that he's felt only once before in his life, and that in a moment of horror.

The Being lifts out an arm. David feels no alarm. The porcelain hand, perfect, glowing white, glowing so brightly that it almost cannot be seen, reaches for him.

David is naked, and the hand, the fingers, touch his naked chest. He feels nothing but the hand is there.

The Being says to him in a Voice that is immortal: "Know. And believe."

David looks down at his chest.

A brand has been burned there, a mark. A five-pointed star within a circle.

He looks up again.

The Beings are gone. There is darkness.

There is Ginny, returned.

Crying. In agony.

She sees him now and she calls to him; she's crying.

"David! Save me! It hurts! Oh, it hurts!"

"Ginny!"

But the wind has her and she's pulled away from him, she struggles.

All is darkness. Darkness.

"Ginny!"

He reaches for her.

She reaches for him and the wind pushes her back toward him.

"Ginny!"

He stretches to touch her—

He stretches—

Stretches—

When you open the door, you don't walk through the door. You will the door to pass around you. The door comes to you. The spirits come to you. The universe comes to you.

Stretches—

And Ginny reaches for him—

Their fingers just touch, touch—

And David screams.

Ginny vanishes. Her flesh melts, her skeleton stands before him, a mockery of Ginny, an unreal Ginny.

The skull grows horns. The skeleton hunches over. Plasma, smoke, ether cover the skull and the skeleton so that before David there stands a demon, a thing, a monster, something foul.

"Ginny!"

The demon smiles and waves its arms. "Life is all! Life is all! Save me!"

"No-oho! *No-ooooo!*"

David screams and screams and in the forever darkness he pulls back his hand, pulls back—

The demon explodes in a wave of green light.

David screams—

And from the green light, exploding, are vomited demons, miniscule green lights, spirits, flying things, coming at him—

Attacking him.

Cheryl awoke in the middle of the night, dreaming of him.

Sensing something.

She sat up in bed startled, not even meaning to think of David.

But she was shuddering, sweating. Shaking.

She turned on the nightstand lamp.

I'm sorry that I can't tell you about it but I'll be back soon, he'd written in the note before he left. *Cheryl, I can't even tell you where I'm going but you'll have to trust me. It's something I have to find out on my own.*

Shaking.

She'd dreamed him, pictured him, seen him screaming for his life in the darkness, falling from the sky, utterly helpless.

She lay back on her pillow.

Son of a bitch . . .

He was screaming on the ground, on the bluff, within his circle, within the tall column of blue light in the middle of the night.

The demons were still there. Surrounding the blue light. Surrounding him.

And David's hand lay outside the blue light of his circle.

Blue hand, shimmering with blue light. He could see it through the mist of light, as though on fire.

He tried to pull it back inside—

And something grabbed it. Something hard and sharp. Held it and wouldn't let go.

Demon.

David yelled.

It had his hand and he tried to pull it back inside, afraid he'd rip it off but afraid of the demon, all the demons.

And the demon's paw, he could see it through the mist of blue light, scaly and shimmering, came inside gripping his hand, breaking through the barrier, his protection.

"Jesus! Let go of me, *let go of me!*"

He wrenched his hand free but the paw was still inside, slapping all over the ground, trying to find him.

While the demons surrounding him tried to push through the barrier. Beaked faces and animal snouts and reptilian masks pushing against the blue curtain of light, stretching it inward as if it were skin, outlining the faces.

"No! Name of God! Agla—! *Ite!*"

He was curled up like a baby trapped in its crib. He grabbed the ritual sword and lifted it up *this is insane insane* and stabbed through the demonic paw once, twice, again and again and again.

Smoke, not blood, erupted from it.

insane insane

David stabbed at it again and severed the paw.

The demonic stump, bleeding smoke, withdrew through the curtain of light, vanishing as though slipping inside a mirror, and the severed paw dissolved, shattered into dust, and the dust blew away in a green fog.

David sobbed and dropped the sword.

He curled up, knees tight *insane insane* and held his burning, painful hand to his chest with his good hand.

Is that how you lost your hand?

Yes. That's how.

God, God, God . . .

He whispered in agony, not sure that whatever spirits there were had heard him, frightened to open his eyes because he might see them breaking through the skinlike barrier of blue light.

They made no noise.

But still he could hear them.

Just as he'd heard his sister's voice.

Just as he'd heard the Being in white speak to him.

Gasping, curled up there, he whispered prayers—

"Ite . . . in nomine Dominus Sabaoth . . . ite ad . . . locus vestrum . . ."

—and though he had his eyes closed and though he couldn't see it, the barrier held, his barrier, his protection, held.

Slowly he felt them fade away, move away like shadows stricken by sunlight as he whispered.

He didn't fall asleep but he was exhausted, and he was wildly strong inside, bursting with energy, but it was a calm energy, something unbelievable.

Godhood, to the ancients.

You will be reborn.

Magic.

Know. And believe.

Wisdom.

Magic . . .

* * *

They found him asleep on the ground, curled up like a baby, his right hand buried under his left arm.

No curtain of blue light.

No magical circle.

Only David on the ground, lit by the first of the sun, the ancient, ancient sun, awake, warming him.

He must have sensed them there, saw them somehow, for he opened his eyes instantly, not startled, and looked up at them.

"David?"

They studied his wide-open eyes.

He had not lost his mind.

In bed, he lay with his right hand resting on a pillowed chair beside him.

As Emma hovered by the door, Gray, kneeling beside the chair, pinched his hand, kneaded it, massaged it.

"Can you feel that?"

"A little."

Gray was disgusted. "Never step outside the circle!" He stood up, face clenched. "You won't lose the hand."

David swallowed, looked away.

Gray moved to Emma. "Warm water and towels. And rest."

"He's done it, Gray."

But he only moved past her, going for the towels.

David turned his head again on the pillow and looked up as Emma came to him. She folded her arms across her breast and looked down at him kindly, perhaps a little awed.

"How are you?"

"It's true, Emma." He was excited, more awake than he'd ever been before. Filled with it, completed by it. "What I saw . . . what I felt! Nothing dies. The whole universe—immortal. With a purpose. A purpose, Emma."

He looked down at his hand.

"I saw my sister. Ginny. It was Ginny. But it changed and—it tricked me. But her spirit was there."

"I know."

"But it was . . . demonic. Mocking me."

"You're at war, David. At war with the evil. The demons. The shadows. They know who you are, now. What you are."

"A Being—a person touched me—"

He was naked and the bedclothes didn't cover him completely; he looked down, but his chest was bare.

"It touched me. There was a mark."

"It won't show here," Emma told him.

He let his head fall back on the pillow, beginning now to feel tired. Drained.

Alive.

"Know," he whispered. "Know, and believe."

Emma decided to let him rest. She went to the door and looked back at him. He was watching her.

"Thank you," she told David.

" 'Thank you'?"

"I'd forgotten. Or I'd never really known. Hoped. I was wrong. About . . . believing. Knowing. There is . . . good."

She had tears in her eyes.

She turned and left him.

David listened to her go away. He closed his eyes, remembered, flexed his hand. He could feel his hand returning.

He slept but, surprisingly, he did not dream.

No Ginny.

No parents.

No demons and no Being in white.

Or if he did dream, he didn't recall it when he awoke.

Night. The damp towel on his hand had grown cool. David sat up and removed it.

His hand felt almost normal. David rubbed his hands together briskly, then pulled on his robe and went down the hall to the bathroom. He took a long shower and dried his hair, then pulled on some clothes and came downstairs.

Gray was in the sitting room. His attitude had improved; he stood up quickly when David reached the bottom of the stairs and addressed him by a formal title.

"Magus." Respectfully.

"Gray."

"How do you feel?"

"Better. Much better."

Gray smiled a little. Maybe Emma had had a talk with him.

"Where's Emma?" David asked him.

"Out on the porch."

He went through the kitchen and opened the back door. Emma was standing on the porch. She didn't turn as he came out.

The back door slammed a little.

The autumn night was very cool. Cold. Emma was wearing a sweater. But though his hair was still a little damp and he wasn't wearing his jacket, David didn't feel the chill.

"When you're rested," Emma told him, "I want you to take a little trip with me."

"Where?"

"About four hours east of here."

"To—?"

Now she faced him. "I want you to know where Theodore Fry came from."

Theodore Fry called again upon Donald Mabrey.

Mabrey was in sour mood.

In his library, he offered Fry a drink. The library was very large. Two walls were filled with bookshelves from floor to ceiling. A tall fireplace and some furniture took up another wall; before the fireplace, which was not lit, which had never been lit, was Mabrey's king-sized desk.

Across from it was his wet bar, the bar itself of imported mahogany. The glass shelves behind were well stocked.

Mabrey poured himself a Scotch.

"Care for one?" he asked Fry, who was sitting in one of the chairs before the fireplace.

"No. Thank you."

"You don't drink much, do you?"

"Not a great deal, no."

Mabrey carried his Scotch around the bar, crossed the room, and stood before Fry. Perhaps trying to intimidate him by his posture.

"Well?"

"It's coming along."

"What does that mean?"

"It's coming along."

"It's been a whole fucking month since I gave you the money and everything."

"We're getting along just fine."

"Jesus."

"It takes time."

'I'm an impatient man. Have you fucked her yet?"

"Oh, yes."

"Jesus," Mabrey said again, and carried his drink to his desk. He sat down, placed the drink before him on his nearly empty desk, rolled the glass between his palms.

Fry stood up and began to peruse some of the books on Mabrey's shelves.

"Have you actually read any of these?"

"Let's talk about Elaine, shall we?"

"There's good material here." Fry took down something and flipped through the pages casually. "She wants to kill you."

"Oh, Jesus Christ!" Mabrey slapped a hand on the desk; the ice in his Scotch clinked. "I was waiting for this, I really was!"

"Were you?"

"What did you tell her?"

"You mean about me? About us?"

"What did you tell her?"

"Not very much. Just enough to keep her interest. She thinks she likes to collect powerful men and then discard them when she's through with them. She thinks she's a black widow spider."

"Jesus Christ, can't you tell me specifically—"

"Oh, relax, Mabrey."

The look in his eyes. Mabrey met it for a moment, then glanced away, disgusted. Nervous.

Fry removed a neatly folded piece of paper from inside his shirt cuff and slipped it into the book he'd borrowed from the shelf. Mabrey didn't notice.

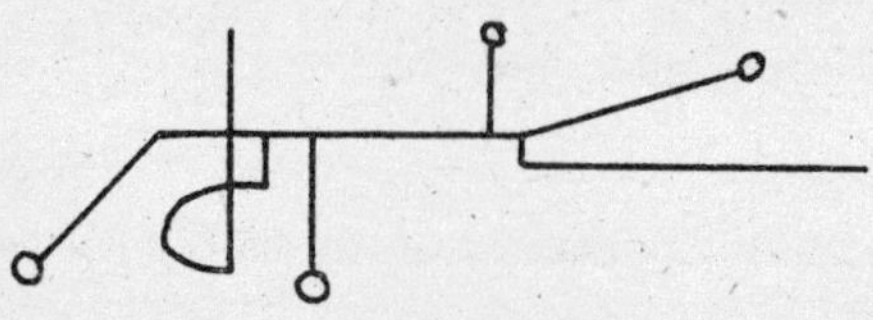

He replaced the book.

"So what does this mean?" Mabrey asked him.

"It doesn't mean a thing."

"You came here to tell me that?"

"Why not?"

"I was hoping for something a little more substantial."

"Well, it's coming along."

"Don't you want any more money?"

"If you have some."

This was absurd. What was it about Fry? Insouciance?

Ego? Carelessness? Simple arrogance? The man was untouchable.

"Don't kill me," Mabrey said, making it sound like a threat.

"I'll need a few more days," Fry told him. "A week, maybe two."

"Does it have to take this long?"

"Yes."

"I want her dead, Mr. Fry. I'm beginning to feel annoyed, and I'm beginning to feel impatient and angry. I think you're playing a game with me."

"I'm playing games with her, not with you. You get to watch."

"That better be all this is," Mabrey told him. "I want to set a deadline." He realized what it sounded like as soon as he'd said it, and he barked a little chuckle. The Scotch. " 'Deadline.' Jesus. When?"

"A week. Within two weeks."

"She's getting to you, isn't she?"

"No. She's not."

"I know what she's like. In public. In bed."

"She said you were still in love with her."

"I can still be in love with her after she's dead."

Fry nodded and smiled a little.

It didn't ease Mabrey's discomfort.

"Here." He opened his desk drawer and took out a brown envelope. He slapped it on the desk.

Fry approached him and picked up the envelope. It was heavy.

"More money," Mabrey told him.

"Money," Fry said.

It was cold and overcast, four hours east of Emma's house.

She and David had driven it in the morning, following some state routes and back roads. He was just beginning to feel hungry and was going to suggest lunch when Emma told him to take a left turn and continue until they came to the gate.

David pulled into a wide blacktop driveway and came to a stop before the tall wrought-iron gate. He was amazed.

It was an estate. A huge, many-storied mansion on top of a brown hill, far away, at the end of the driveway, far beyond the iron gate. Wide roaming lawns, dappled now with fallen leaves. Trees everywhere. A stone wall surrounding everything, enclosing everything, fronting woods that were deep and dark.

He got out of the car and walked forward to the gate, gripped the iron bars.

Emma came up behind him.

"This is his?"

"Not anymore. It was in his family for seventy-five years."

"He was born here?"

"His grandfather built it. Money from the old country. They used to be Freye—*e-y-e*. Ted never married. He was an only child. The whole family died out, and when some old aunt died she left it to him."

"God, look at it. Nobody lives like this anymore."

"There were debts. Ted didn't care about it, so he sold the estate."

"A spoiled little rich boy," David said.

"He lived here until he was twenty-five. Then he sold it and traveled the world."

"Can we get in?"

"There's nothing in there," Emma told him. "I think the county owns it now. There's nothing in there. Furniture." She told him, "The whole family didn't practice magic, you know."

He looked at her.

"There's no reason to go in. But I wanted you to see this. The woods over there?" She pointed.

"Yes."

"When he was a little boy he built an altar of stones back there. He used to sacrifice animals. Yes. Like Abraham sacrificing Isaac."

"He told you that?"

"See the big tree over there? The oak."

David saw it. It was huge.

"It's hollow inside. When he was a boy he'd sit inside that tree. It was his hiding place. He was so frightened of the world that he'd hide in there. Once he ran away from home and slept in it all night."

"Fry. Afraid."

"He sat in it one evening during a thunderstorm. Daring the lightning to strike the tree and burn him alive. Daring God."

Light drops struck David's face.

Emma said, "It's raining."

He was staring at the tree, imagining it.

"Come on, David."

He looked back at her. "He brought you out here—showed you this . . . Was he in love with you, Emma?"

"I don't know."

"People know."

"David—"

"But you loved him."

"I don't know if it was love or some kind of fascination." She paused as if to say something more, but—"Come on."

She led the way back down the drive to the car. As they got inside, thunder boomed heavily and the light drizzle suddenly became a downpour.

"He knows we're here," David said. Not quite smiling.

He moved to start his car but Emma put a hand on his to stop him. She was staring out the windshield, staring at the sheets of rain pouring down the gray glass.

It was stuffy in the car.

"You must do it, David."

"Kill him."

"Exterminate him. Abolish him. Make it as though he'd never existed. Because there's something no one knows but me."

He felt a little thrill deep in his stomach.

Emma looked him in the eyes. "The sigil you drew? The sigil of Bezemoth?"

"What about it?"

"When Ted felt that he'd learned enough—when he wished to sever his connection with this world entirely—he wanted to go beyond what anyone else had ever done. David . . . he performed a ritual and sacrificed himself to Bezemoth."

"He committed suicide?"

"Fry is immortal. He has the soul of a demon. Bezemoth was—is—a medieval spirit. Older than that. It hasn't been on the earth in a thousand years."

"Do you know what you're saying, Emma?"

"You want to kill him, and the man you want to kill is already dead."

It was storming outside Elaine Mabrey's home. The home Donald had bought for her, hoping it would pave the way toward an amicable divorce.

She and Fry were lying naked in bed, sipping wine, looking at the rain and the blowing gray trees outside the picture window. There was a fire going in the fireplace across from them.

"He built this house for you?"

"What did he *say*?" Elaine wanted to know.

"It looks like his library. Only you have a bed instead of a desk and you don't have any books."

"I don't like books. Books are old. I don't like to read. What did he *say*?"

"He didn't say anything."

"Did you do whatever it was you said you were going to do?"

He touched her hair. "What are you afraid of?"

"I'm not afraid of anything."

"Liar."

"I'm not."

"Just remember," Fry cautioned her, "I'm not going to keep you around forever. I'm dangerous."

"I'm dangerous, too. Maybe I won't keep you around." She pressed herself against him; wine spilled from her glass and she licked it from his chest and nipples. "What did you mean when you said that I've never not been alive?"

"Just that."

"Isn't that what you said?"

"Yes."

"You mean, dead?"

"When a magician practices sorcery, he kills himself and brings himself back to life."

"Or herself."

"It's a spiritual death. Spiritual rebirth."

"Is that what we're going to do when we kill Donald?"

"No."

"You just want me because I'm a good whore and you haven't had it so good in a long time."

"Absolutely."

"I like being your whore."

"You like it for the time being."

She smiled at him, set her wine on the nightstand and jumped out of bed quickly and walked across the room. Nude and deliberate.

On the mantel above the fireplace was a framed picture of Donald.

"I suppose you want to know why I have this here," Elaine said to Fry.

"I know why."

"Why?"

"You sit up in bed and jerk off and swear at him while you're doing it."

She laughed intricately. "Maybe I do. Maybe I do." She studied the picture. "This is all you need?"

"It helps."

"Make an invocation," she said. "Call down your spirits." She took hold of the picture and turned quickly, hair flying, and smashed it against the fireplace. Fry laughed. Glass shattered over the brick and the carpeting.

Elaine threw the broken metal frame into the fireplace and held up Donald's picture with two hands.

"Go to hell, you son of a bitch!"

She ripped it in half and threw the pieces into the fire.

Then she came back across the room, wincing a little, and threw herself on the bed so that her head was next to Fry's feet and her feet beside his face.

"Look. I must've stepped on some glass. I'm bleeding."

He took her feet and licked the blood from them, taking his time.

The rain and the storm and the lightning had followed them back, so that in the evening the rain pattered on the kitchen window as David sat at the table, coffee beside him, some books before him, and paper and pencil.

And a map, a road atlas of the northeastern states.

He was drawing the Bezemoth sigil over and over again, in different sizes, and staring at the road atlas, marking it up.

Gray came in.

"It's getting late, David."

"We don't know where Fry is," David said, "but we know where he's been. We know where he's killed people. Look."

He pointed to the road atlas. He'd circled the cities where he knew Fry had been and connected them with lines.

"Good Lord . . ."

"It fits," David said. "Wherever he goes, wherever he moves—he's drawing the sigil of Bezemoth." He smiled, feeling pleased with himself, and looked up at Gray. "He may not even know he's doing it. Maybe his demon's doing it."

Gray went to the doorway and called into the sitting room. "Emma!"

"It fits," David said. "It fits, it fits."

When she came in, Gray nodded to the table. Emma leaned over David's shoulder, and David tapped the road atlas. "Bezemoth's sigil."

"My God. Of course. Fry's caught in it. It's caught here, on the earth, with us. Gray! All it can do is wander! It's trapped!"

"He's in one of these cities," David predicted. "But we don't know which one. And if he's with anyone— if he's there to kill—we have no idea who his victim is."

They used the circular table in the sitting room. Emma set out two black sheets of paper and a white piece of chalk. Simple construction paper. They turned out the lights and the three of them held hands around the table.

"By Arnamon and by Elgiel, by Sath and the holy Names of Elohim—you are bound to this place and bound to us. Reveal!"

Emma repeated it. David and Gray echoed her.

"We command it by Arnamon and by Elgiel! Reveal to us, reveal!"

The white piece of chalk rolled.

Rolled, and settled still.

"Reveal!"

Rolled, and stood up on one end, on top of the black paper.

And began to write.

The chalk scratched out letters slowly and carefully, one by one.

"We command it by Arnamon and Elgiel!"

When it was finished the chalk fell again to the table and shuddered.

David read what the chalk, what whatever spirit had guided the chalk, had written:

"EDGARTONEMABREYDMABREY. It doesn't make any sense."

"Edgarton," Gray told him. "Emabrey. D-mabrey. Mabrey. That's the name. An E. Mabrey and a D. Mabrey. Two people."

Emma looked at David. "Did you circle someplace named Edgarton on your map?"

"Edgar*town*. Edgartown, Pennsylvania."

He didn't sleep that night.

He lay awake and thought of—everything.

Everything.

Late, Emma looked in on him, opening the door and leaning against it.

"Get some sleep."

"I don't know if I can do it, Emma."

"But you can, David."

"I don't know if— It should take years."

"You were born with it."

Was I?

"Was I?"

"Good Lord." She opened the door wider, moving to come in, but David told her:

"No. Thanks. I'm okay."

"All right."

She closed the door quietly, and David listened to her footsteps go away and go quiet.

He got out of bed. Opened his window curtains so that he could see the cloudy night, the silhouetted skeletons of trees, the frost on the glass.

He crossed his arms upon his chest, pressed his palms together, raised his hands above his forehead, and held out his arms.

"In nomine Sabaoth, Spiritus Magnus, suscipe me, o omnipotens aeterne, Spiritus . . ."

He prayed.

Prayed as all sorcerers and magicians pray, have ever prayed.

Calling up the light within him.

Visualizing, revisiting the astral plane, the Being in white—

Know. And believe.

And as David prayed his doubts went away, his strength returned, warmth filled him, he touched himself again, his universe deep within him.

All was made clear again.

Purpose, his purpose.

Kill him.

Restore a balance that had become unbalanced. Separate the evil from the pained flesh that housed it. Call down the light.

When he returned to bed he fell asleep quickly and rested soundly.

Magician.

Gray had his car packed for him the next morning when David, freshly showered and dressed, came downstairs and went out onto the back porch. He was carrying his jacket; the morning was cool so he pulled it on.

Emma and Gray were standing in the driveway beside his car.

God, he'd been here over a month, he'd come here as an angry, confused man wanting to—what? Help his sister who was dead? Kill Fry? Just know?

He'd just wanted to *know*.

He walked down into the driveway.

"Magus."

He nodded to Gray.

Gray held out his hand and David took it.

"This seems too sudden," David said.

Emma smiled, rather sadly.

"I can't thank you with words," he told Gray. "I'll just have to thank you by whatever I can do."

"Dominus vobiscum, David."

Emma embraced him.

"Will I ever see you again?" he asked her.

"Perhaps. What matters is that we've learned from one another, you and I. That's what matters. Thank you."

"I will come back, you know."

"If you wish."

"I'll bring Cheryl."

Emma smiled and nodded.

There was nothing more to say. Nothing more to do here. The teachers, the student— He'd never felt this way before. It was almost like saying goodbye to his parents, and he'd never had the opportunity to say goodbye to his parents.

He got into his car, feeling awkward but strong inside, and he started it, rolled down the window.

"Goodbye," David told them, looking at them, and started the engine and moved down the driveway.

He didn't look in his rearview mirror.

"He'll do it," Gray said, watching him go.

"He'll succeed." Emma took one of his hands and pressed it strongly. "He'll destroy a great evil, this . . . son that I never had."

Part III

BEZEMOTH IPSISSIMUS

Evening.

Mabrey was spending it drinking.

He was sitting in his library with the lights off, the drapes drawn, so that everything was gray and dim and hidden. But he knew his way around.

The bottle was on top of the imported mahogany bar, and as Mabrey finished he-didn't-know-how-many-this-one-was, he got up and went to the bar and poured himself another, this time almost emptying the Scotch bottle.

What the hell, empty it.

He drank his Scotch straight.

Because tonight something didn't feel right. Just didn't feel right.

Mabrey knew it, sensed it.

Something in the air. Gray and dim and hidden, maybe hiding here in his library.

He went back to his desk and sat down, put his glass of Scotch on the desk and turned on the lamp. He looked at his hands, he didn't know why. He looked at his glass of Scotch. He was alone here, in the darkness, in this little pool of yellow light at his desk.

''Donald Mabrey?''

Startled, he looked up.

Something in the air had come to life.

And someone walked toward him from a corner of his library. Young man. Kind of tall. Wearing a jacket. Nobody.

"Who the hell are you? How did you get in here?" He felt himself standing up, leaning on the desk. Very angry.

"My name is Trevisan.". From the shadows. "David Trevisan."

"How the hell did you get in here?"

"Do you know Theodore Fry?"

"Jesus!"

"Do you?"

"That's none of your goddamn—"

"He was here. I can feel it. He's an extremely dangerous man, Mr. Mabrey. Do you know what he is?"

"I know what he is. What the hell are *you*?"

"I'm a dangerous man, too. Who's E. Mabrey? Your wife?"

"Jesus, what is this?"

"A relative? A brother?"

"Jesus." But he didn't move, he stayed behind the desk, talking to this young man in his home, his own home.

"If you're involved with Theodore Fry, you may not have a great deal of time left. Do you understand what I'm saying?"

"I want you to—"

"You're going to have to talk with me. Now. Tell me who E. Mabrey is."

Mabrey swallowed thickly. Unable to stand any longer, feeling shaky, he sank back down into his chair. "My wife."

"Your wife."

"Elaine."

"Did you hire Theodore Fry to kill your wife?"

"I don't have to tell you anything! Jesus Christ, who—"

"All you have to tell me is where your wife is now. I'm here for Fry."

"Who the hell are you?"

"I've told you that."

"Another one like him?"

"Tell me where your wife is, Mr. Mabrey."

"I don't know. All right? I don't know."

"Do you really know what he is? Do you really think he'd let you walk away from something like this?"

Mabrey thought about that. He reconsidered. He'd been reconsidering ever since the afternoon on the patio. He said, "Not me? You're not here for me? Just him? Just Elaine?"

Silence . . .

"I bought her a house," he admitted. "Out in Darrow."

"The address."

"Do you know where that is?"

"Give me the address."

"I don't remember the address. It's just past the crossroads. Commons and Burford. Tudor place. It's . . . exclusive out there."

David stepped forward, reaching inside his jacket.

Mabrey leaned back in his chair. His right hand closed around the glass of Scotch; he wondered if he could use it as a weapon, maybe throw the Scotch in his face and smash the glass on his head.

But what David Trevisan removed from inside his jacket was a piece of jewelry.

He dropped it on Mabrey's desk.

A talisman on a chain.

What he and Long had gone through. The same thing. Different, now, but the same thing.

An underground world of sorcerers, and once in a while ordinary people get hurt . . .

"Wear this."

"What is it?"

"Wear it. And pray. There are things out there—they may listen."

He moved around the desk and headed for the tall entrance doors.

Mabrey stood up again. "Look! Wait! I'll go with you!"

David paused and turned as he was going, and warned him, "For the good of your own soul, Mabrey—stay the hell away from it."

"Why do you do things like this?" she asked him.

"Because I can," Fry told her. "Because all human beings are dirty little animals living in pain. Because I've seen the other side, and it's better."

They were in Elaine's living room. They'd moved the furniture against the walls and pulled up the carpet. They'd left a table in the center of the room; Fry had placed his tools on it. And he'd drawn a wide circle in black chalk around the table, around Elaine and himself.

He was in a black robe. Elaine was adjusting hers. She was nervous.

"Better," she said. "Better for him?"

"I suppose."

"And—for me?"

Very nervous.

"No one escapes, sooner or later."

"You?" she asked.

"Yes. I've escaped."

David found the crossroads. Commons and Burford. Mabrey was right: It was isolated out here, the houses wide apart, past even the rural gas stations, closed this late at night, past the few old farmhouses that remained.

He nearly drove by her house. Hit the brakes. Leaned across the front seat and rolled down the passenger side window so that he could be sure. Because there was a house back there, but no lights on, it was hard to judge what kind of house it might be. Tudor?

He backed up and turned into the driveway. He turned out his lights.

The driveway curved around, and he had a clear view of the house in the darkness.

Tudor.

The candles, glowing, were arranged on the table. The large brass bowl had been filled with incense.

Fry lit another wooden match and handed it to Elaine.

"Light the incense."

She hesitated. The match quivered so strongly in her hand that she nearly extinguished the flame.

"Light the incense, Elaine."

"I'm nervous."

"You're terrified."

He took her hand, gripped it. She winced. He hurt her.

He moved her hand forward so that the fiery end of the match dipped into the brass bowl. The incense began to glow, began to smoke.

Aromatic fumes lifted.

"Repeat after me. Veni, Bezemoth Ipsissimus."

"Veni, Bezemoth Ipsissimus . . ."

He got out of his car and didn't even close his door, but left it partly open. No noise.

Above him, far away, he heard the first of the low thunder coming.

Energy, collecting.

None of the front windows was lit, but off to one side of the house David could see yellow light, faint yellow light—candlelight—reflected on the grass.

He stepped up onto the front porch. It was flanked on both sides by tall, ornamented columns. The front door was two doors, swinging open in the middle.

David took in a deep breath.

He pressed his palms together before his chest, raised them to his forehead.

"Agla. Sabaoth. Ator. Enor."

He pushed his palms against the doors, the seam between them where they opened.

"Aeior!"

Fry heard the door crash inward.

Elaine, beside him, jerked up her head. "Donald!"

She began to move.

"Donald!"

Fry was quick. He gripped her forearm and pulled Elaine back so roughly that she was nearly twisted to her knees.

"It's Donald! It's Donald!"

"It is not Donald!"

The sound of the falling doors sank away, but thunder, moving in above the sky, seemed to carry the echo.

They heard footsteps.

Coming toward them.

Fry's grip tightened.

"Donal—"

But Fry held her so strongly that her call ended in a moan.

The footsteps approached slowly. Carefully.

Fry waited.

No demon . . .

Just beyond the open living room entrance he saw a rippling shadow, a shadow only somewhat darker than the floor itself.

Demons cast no shadows.

And the owner of the shadow came into view.

Elaine gasped.

He stood before them, framed by the entranceway, staring at them, no look of shock or surprise on his face.

"You," Fry said.

David remained still.

"The priest."

"A *priest?*"

"It's over, Fry. Elaine—don't move. Stay where you are."

"Who are you? Ted, who *is* he?"

David raised his arms and crossed them at the wrists.

Fry smiled. "Where have you learned this?"

"Who is he? *Who is he?*"

More thunder came.

Fry let go of Elaine. "Stay!"

She didn't try to escape.

He lowered his head intently, like an animal eyeing its prey, and crossed his own wrists, held his fists up before him.

"I know," he said. "Only she could have taught you this. Only she."

Elaine moaned, "Who is he?"

"I congratulate you, priest. You survived my sending. You survived my dog. How have you found me here?"

"Your demon draws its symbol as you travel."

Fry growled.

David said, "Elaine?"

It was all in his voice.

Run.

She looked quickly at Fry, edged away from him, glanced at David, lurched to run free.

But already Fry had read her mind.

He brought down an arm, driving his elbow into her side. Something snapped; a rib. Elaine gasped quickly and, grabbing her side, fell to the floor, her knees cracking loudly.

"Elaine!"

"Fool," Fry said to him, crossing his arms again.

The lights in the living room flickered on and off. The thunder came closer.

Fry screamed.

And David, not prepared, was struck by a sudden, violent, rushing wind. It filled the room. It pushed him back. It hurled him toward the living room entrance.

He tried to bend low. But the wind—Fry's wind—shoved him into the wall. David threw out his arms to support himself. The back of his head hit the wood paneling, and his legs buckled and he dropped.

He forced himself up, brought his arms before him again.

The furniture piled on either side of the room creaked and groaned in the sudden wind. Two chairs and a table were knocked free. They smashed loudly to the floor.

The lights continued to flicker on and off.

Sprawled on the floor, half within the black circle and half without, Elaine lay on her side and whimpered. The wind clutched at her robe; in embarrassment she tried to push it back around her body.

Fry, standing above her, trembled.

He screamed again.

David, leaning back against the wall and on his feet again, kept his wrists crossed and resisted.

The wind came, roaring, exploding around the room, and David stood against it.

Fry grunted.

The bowl of smoking incense was torn from the table. The candles were knocked over and pulled into the air.

They spun around the room, throwing wet wax, and hot ashes flew from the brass bowl. Candles landed on wooden furniture, and behind Fry and Elaine the drapes caught fire.

Fry howled.

The wind, the thunder—

David, sweating, fell to his knees.

"In nomine—"

And Fry came ahead. Grabbing the table with one hand, he lifted it and threw it aside, held his fists up before him and howled.

Arcs of snapping electricity erupted in the room. Green light, crackling and smoking. Jumping from the walls to the floor, from the ceiling to the furniture.

Striking David.

He shrieked.

"By God, Fry, no more, *no more!*"

He pushed on one leg, fighting the wind, fighting the pain of etheric lightning, forcing himself forward.

"No more!"

The lights went dark, came on, flickered off, on—

Elaine tried to crawl away, but she was in agony.

Behind her the drapes were completely aflame, hanging in shreds and sending waves of smoke across the ceiling.

Elaine fell onto her back and began to cry. She saw David sinking to his knees, dressed in a green bath of fire, green smoke.

Priest . . .

And the priest, finding energy, finding hate, finding strength, something within himself, pulled himself to his feet again and roared, screamed like a maniac and threw out his arms, pointed them—

And Fry howled.

And dropped back.

A bolt of something, green light or green fire, struck him and exploded in sparks around him, in waves.

Elaine laughed. Her laugh turned into a cough, and she grabbed her side and winced and kicked her legs.

Because Fry was in pain and the priest—the priest had a look of rage in his eyes, a kind of madness.

She closed her eyes, shivered her head, opened her eyes, and saw David.

Saw someone beside him, coming through the entrance-way into the living room.

"Donal—!"

He didn't even see her, there on the floor, through the smoke and the flames. Or if he did, he didn't care.

"Fry!"

He had a gun.

"Do—"

The gun exploded. Little flames reached out from it, like jumping orange tongues.

Elaine heard Fry roar, high above her.

David yelled, "Mabrey!"

And Donald was gone. In an instant. Like the priest, covered and swallowed by a green haze, green fire.

Only the priest had known how to protect himself.

Donald, shrieking, completely on fire, writhed and rolled on the floor, wrapped in crawling ropes of flame.

There was a loud explosion, a crash of some kind.

Elaine, whimpering, turned her head—

The wall behind her, the drapes and the wall itself, all fiery, crashed down upon her.

She felt the heat, closed her eyes—

From where he stood, David, on the other side of the living room, saw the wall crumple and collapse, taking half the ceiling with it, burying Elaine and Fry.

She hadn't even had time to scream.

Fry hadn't even had time to protect himself.

Gasping, David pushed himself away from the billowing flames and pouring smoke. Back through the entranceway.

He limped down the hallway and into the foyer, jumped across the fallen front doors, and hurried into the cold autumn night.

Trees were blowing outside. Thunder still groaned in the sky but it wasn't loud, now.

David didn't even make it to his car.

He fell in the driveway, collapsed, and rolled onto his back. A light drizzle touched him, washed him, seemed to cool the fever in him. It grew into a rain.

Still he lay there. He closed his eyes. He felt as though he were dissolving in the rain.

Could Fry have lived through it?

Could his demon have lived through it?

Mabrey had been killed instantly. Elaine had never had a chance. But Fry—

He heard sirens.

Someone call the police?

David opened his eyes.

The sky was orange, as bright as dawn.

He sat up. The whole house was on fire. The whole house, screaming and twisting, threatening to collapse.

David got to his feet, feeling the pain. As if there were a demon inside himself now, playing maliciously with him. Pinching his muscles with iron-hot nails. Kicking at him from inside, biting and poking.

He reached into his jacket pocket, hoping to God that his car keys hadn't fallen out inside the house.

He found them and got into his car.

But he couldn't leave. Not until he knew Fry was dead. Truly dead. Exterminated. As though he had never been. The demon—gone.

He started his car and drove it forward, steered onto the lawn, and pulled behind Elaine's garage. He parked, got out, and walked dazedly until he came to a side door. He kicked it in. Never knowing where the strength came from to do it.

He closed the door behind him and felt his way forward, past a car, until he reached the garage door. It had a window. dow.

David watched out the window.

The burning house.

The arriving fire trucks.

The rainstorm.

The collapsing house.

Armies of men in shining black.

Ambulances. Police. Paramedics.

Moving like an army.

The hoses, shooting water.

Until the dawn came.

Until, with the dawn, the fire trucks left, and the paramedics (with two charred bodies; David couldn't identify them), and the police.

Until David, in a dream, came out of the garage and walked, stumbling, toward the smoking ruins of the house.

Fallen walls. Everything charred, all black, reduced to charcoal and ashes. Timbers. Brick and stone.

Silence and ashes and death.

As if a pocket of hell had forced itself up from underneath the earth and exploded into flames on contact with the air. And this was all that was left, a crater filled with rubble.

He stood there for a long time, for what seemed like a long time, until the sun came up.

No Fry.

No Fry.

He was buried there, the demon was dead, he'd been buried alive and burned to death, released, the demon was lying dead and black, its spirit turned to waste, buried in the hell of a burning house, crushed beneath it.

David walked back to his car behind the garage, got in, and started it up.

He found the strength to drive, the strength to stay on the road and find a motel.

And when he'd paid for his room he locked the door and tore off his clothes and climbed into bed and slept the entire day.

In the silence and ashes and death, from the rubble and charred timber and the bricks and stones, the ruined house made a noise.

The ruined house shuddered in the cold, coming back to life.

One brick fell.

Clacking.

And, after a moment, another brick fell.

A black length of wood was pushed aside.

And a hand appeared.

Long fingers, stained skin, reaching, feeling, grabbing hold of anything.

And another hand.

Shuddering, shaking, the fingers, the hands found strength, gripped warm wood, pulled up.

The face.

The head lifted into view.

Alive.

Alive.

Outside, the cool late autumn continued to rain, and in the afternoon the rain became snow.

The heater kicked on in the motel room.

The sky darkened outside the window.

And still David slept, so completely and profoundly that he never turned in the bed or rolled over.

I don't think I really wanted to become a priest. I think I just wanted to hide for a while.

She wanted to communicate with the spirit world. She wanted to talk to your dead parents.

There's this whole underground out there . . . Like a religion nobody knows about.

Magic is an art of solitude, but you must never believe that you're ever completely alone.

By God, Fry, no more, no more!

Help! Me! David! They're . . . eating . . . me!

He sat up in bed, trembling.

Awake.

"Gin—"

A dream.

Dreams . . .

He sank back.

The room was very dark, very dark.

He looked at the clock on the nightstand beside the bed.

Late in the evening Emma looked outside the kitchen window and noticed that the snow had let up. And she heard something.
Not the wind.
Coming up the driveway.
Headlights swept across the trees, and Emma saw a long, dark automobile climb past the house, heard it come to a stop.
She yelled into the sitting room. "Gray!"
He was there quickly—the sound of her voice—standing in the doorway. "Emma, what?"
"He's come back."
"David?"
"He's come back!"
Gray said nothing. He crossed the kitchen and reached into a side closet, took out his heavy jacket, and pulled it on. He opened the back door and stepped out onto the porch.
Emma leaned against the kitchen counter and didn't move, closed her eyes . . .
Gray walked across the porch, boots cracking on the frost, the snow. He gripped the porch rail, looked down into the driveway.
He was standing there, tall, in a coat. Breathing steam. Just touched by the light coming from the kitchen window.
Gray said, "So."
Fry bowed. "Magister."
"You slander me by calling me that."
"The student surpasses the teacher."
"I curse myself every morning for teaching you anything."
"Moralist."
"But I've trained the man to kill you, Fry."

"The priest?" He laughed lightly. "Then he's your second disappointment."

"No . . ."

"Oh, yes." Fry stepped forward. "You seem shocked."

Gray didn't say anything.

"Is Emma in there?"

"Yes."

"I want to see her."

"I can't let you do that."

Fry moved. Brought up his arms, called out a word.

And Gray moved.

Not quickly enough.

By early evening David had showered and dressed and repacked his car. Not in a hurry. But he'd decided not to return to Noland.

He'd promised Emma that he'd come back with Cheryl. Have a nice dinner together, was his thought. He'd explain to Cheryl what had happened and she'd understand. She would have to, because it was true, this was him, now, and she'd have to accept it.

Cheryl was in love with him, and he was certainly in love with her. And he'd hurt her, disappointed her. And he would correct that because he could correct that.

But he couldn't go back to her now. He wasn't done yet.

Maybe it was because he hadn't actually seen Fry's body.

Maybe it was because everything that had happened with Emma and Gray was apart from Cheryl.

But David wanted it to be completely finished, put aside in a locked box somehow, before returning to Cheryl, returning to his home.

Before going back home.

He stopped at a small diner about an hour after leaving the motel. It offered breakfast twenty-four hours a day, and since he'd slept all day the thought of eggs and toast and sausage sounded good, so he had breakfast.

The snow let up while he was eating, but once David got back on the road, driving northeast on state roads toward New York, flurries started again.

He stopped twice again during the night to have his thermos filled with coffee.

About three hours before dawn, just as he was crossing into New York state, David was playing with the radio, trying to get a clear station, when static came in. Loud. He twisted the knob back and forth, glancing up at the road as he did so, steering one-handed. Shiny black road, wet fallen snow, patches of ice.

His car headlights began to dim.

For Christ's—

They went out.

David hit the brakes almost too hard. He nearly slid off the road.

The headlights came back on, but flickered. Off and on, off and on.

And the static on the radio grew so loud that he snapped the radio off.

The static continued.

His car began to rattle and chug, threatening to stall.

Jesus. The battery? Can't be overheated. Must be the bat—

In the sky above him, in the darkness, above the long deserted middle-of-the-night road, he saw a light. Green light.

Moving toward him.

"Jesus Christ!"

No one else in sight. Ditches on both sides of the road, surrounded by trees. And the green light, coming toward him very quickly, filling the sky. A ghost image. A mirage.

A face.

Eyes—nose—mouth—

Filling the sky.

Fry.

David planted his foot on the brake; if a wind struck, maybe that would keep his car on the side of the road. He let go of the steering wheel and brought up his arms, crossed at the wrists.

Priest! You've murdered her, priest!

He kept his head bent low, eyes closed tightly. Still he saw the brilliant green light through his eyelids.

The words were in his brain. Not spoken, but there, he heard them.

And the loud static went silent.

The green light disappeared; his eyes went black.

David looked up and slowly lowered his arms.

Dark night sky. Ditches on both sides of the road, surrounded by trees.

He put his trembling hands on the steering wheel, gripped the wheel so strongly he thought his finger bones would snap.

His headlights were on.

He was sweating. He rolled down his window, and the cold night air hit him like a wall.

God, God, God . . .

A sudden light attacked him from behind, flashed in his rearview mirror, and David—"*Jesus Christ!*"—jumped in his seat again.

The car went around him, the driver slowing down to take a look at him.

God, God, God. Was it real? What did it mean?

Fry?

God, why shouldn't it be real?

Dawn.

The first thing he saw was the porch.

He stared at it as he came to a stop in Emma's driveway. Opened his door, got out.

And the trees. On either side of the porch the trees were down. Snapped at their bases. The porch roof was collapsed and tilted crazily, one splintered end of it resting on the ground.

There were signs of fire—charred black streaks on the walls of the porch, the side of the house. Windows were broken.

David started walking forward.

The screen door opened.

Emma.

David stopped.

She was dressed in a tattered housecoat. That was all. Her feet were bare, and she was standing in the snow. The screen door slammed loudly behind her and Emma came to the top of the porch steps, her head almost bumping the buckled roof.

"Emma?"

His impulse was to run up the stairs, but the look in her eyes, her expression—

"Can't you stop him?" she whispered. "Even you?"

He could barely hear her. "Emma?"

She started to fall; she leaned against the porch wall and eased herself down so that she was huddled there. She kicked snow away with her bare feet.

She began to cry. "Can't even you stop him?"

David came up the steps and sat down carefully beside her. Emma leaned toward him; David wound his arms about her. She was trembling fiercely.

"Emma, what happened?"

"He killed Gray! There's nothing left! I have to bury him!" She pushed him away, tears running down her face. "He's all burned and there's nothing left! I have to bury him!"

"When, Emma? When?"

She stood up again, backing away from David, shivering in the cold. David got to his feet.

"He wouldn't kill me!" Emma screamed at him. "I begged him to! He promised me he would! But he wouldn't kill me! I want to die! And he wouldn't kill me!"

"Emma!"

"I begged him to! And he wouldn't!"

David moved away from her. Back down the steps.

Emma yelled to him from the porch, "Couldn't you stop him? Couldn't even you stop him? Gray couldn't! Couldn't you drive faster in your fucking car? What's the matter with you? Don't you know what he is?"

"Where did he go, Emma?"

"He's not a man!" she screamed. *"Couldn't you stop him?"*

"Where did he go, Emma?"

Her voice fell to a whisper again. "Where do you think he went? He wants you, now."

"Oh, God."

"He wants you, now, David. Where do you think he went?"

She'd had a rotten day and it was going to be a rotten evening. Gray all day, rainy and snowy. Her apartment was cold, and Cheryl had turned the heat up but not too far. Astronomical heating bills. She still felt cold.

She told herself to dig out her sweaters and put one on, but she was washing the dishes and she didn't want to.

The doorbell.

Great.

Amy from work.

Was she going to come over this evening?

What happened to that guy you were seeing? The one with the sister?

Amy, I really don't want to talk about it.

Well, if you don't want to tell me, what is it, your big secret or something?

The doorbell rang again.

Cheryl swore and dried her hands on a dishtowel, crossed the living room, glanced at the TV news, opened the door.

"Miss D'Angelo?"

It took her a moment. "Mr.—*Fry?*"

"Your boyfriend," he told her, placing a hand on the door. "David? You and I have a serious problem on our hands, Miss D'Angelo. He's been chasing me all over the country, trying to kill me."

He drove. As furiously fast as he could.

All day long, stopping only when he had to, through New York, through northern Pennsylvania, concentrating, mentally forcing himself ahead, going, going.

Cheryl . . .

He was alive, Fry was alive, the *demon* in Fry that hadn't ever died, the *demon* in Fry that killed and moved and was alive, immortal.

Don't you know what he is?

He wasn't a man. He was a demon. Some spirit, life form playing games, happily on earth to kill and leave its trail behind it like slime from some crawling reptile. How many people had it killed in the Middle Ages?

Who the hell had put the genie back in its bottle until Fry had opened it again?

Nothing, he knew nothing, there was nothing there.

Would he have killed it if Mabrey hadn't interfered?

What was he killing? Fry? Bezemoth?

He drove, he drove . . .

Would Fry simply kill Cheryl?

Hold her hostage?

Fry would go to Cheryl, of course, because that was

the most obvious way of drawing David out, of forcing him into a confrontation.

And this was their game, now. He'd inherited it from Long, from Emma and Gray.

Think, think . . .

What will he do?

What would I do?

He drove, he drove . . .

Could he draw the circle, raise his hands, call up the universe within him, and slay something that couldn't be slain?

He wasn't killing Fry.

Fry had killed himself a long time ago.

He was trying to kill a demon.

Or—was he trying to kill a demon?

What was he trying to do?

Think, think . . .

What would he do when he stood there, facing Fry, facing this demon clothed in Fry's body? What would he do?

What could he do?

She'd let him in. No way she couldn't have done that. And they'd sat there for a while and talked. Cheryl hadn't made supper yet, and she didn't feel comfortable with Fry there, she didn't want to offer him a meal, she didn't *like* him. He'd done something to Ginny, whatever it might have been. Cheryl didn't like him.

They sat there. The TV was on. Fry didn't watch the TV. He watched Cheryl, glanced at the magazines she had lying about, *Cosmopolitan* and *Savvy.*

Eight-thirty.

"Mr. Fry, are you going to stay here all evening?"

"No, no. I'm waiting for David to show up."

"I really don't want you here all night."

"Well, I think he'll be coming along shortly."

He'd told her his side of the story, and Cheryl had mulled it over while finishing the dishes, and she'd told Fry that she didn't know where David was and hadn't heard from him in several weeks, almost two months, in fact.

"Why don't you give me a phone number or something, and if he comes I'll tell him to call you."

"I don't think you understand. This is very serious."

"It sure is. I'm going to ask you to leave."

"Not just yet."

Good Lord, he was going to refuse to leave?

What was he going to do, just stay here?

"I have to go to work tomorrow," Cheryl told him.

Fry just looked at her.

Was he deaf? What the hell was going on here?

It occurred to her that Amy from work would've been pleasant company tonight.

Cheryl got up and went into the kitchen, reached for the phone.

"Who're you calling?"

She turned around quickly, finger in the dial. He was right behind her.

"My girlfriend from work."

"Don't."

"You're making me very nervous, Mr. Fry."

"I suppose that's inevitable. I have that effect on some people."

The phone buzzed loudly in her hand.

"Hang up the phone, Cheryl."

She did. "What're you going to do?" she asked him, trying to sound as forceful as she could. "You going to rape me?"

"Of course not. We're just going to sit here and wait. This is very important to me."

"It's important to me that I— I don't want people I don't know sitting around in my apartment like they own the place."

"Let's go back into the living room."

"I have to go to the bathroom."

She moved past him, careful not to touch him, even brush his arm, and went down the hall.

He followed her.

She tried to close the bathroom door, but Fry held it open.

"Jesus Christ!" Cheryl screamed at him. "I'm only going to the fucking bathroom! Will you give me some fucking privacy?"

He let her close the door, but Cheryl knew he was standing right there, on the other side.

She sat there for a long time, trying to relax. Embarrassed because this maniac was listening to every little sound she made.

When she was done she washed her hands—they were shaking—and opened the door and looked him in the eyes.

"You're not a nice man, Mr. Fry."

"I know that."

"I think you're some kind of pervert."

"I'm not a pervert."

They returned to the living room. He took his place on the couch; Cheryl sat in a chair.

She couldn't watch TV. Couldn't read a magazine. This was insane. She looked over at him.

"Everything David said about you is true, isn't it?"

"What did he say about me?"

"And everything he was afraid of—this witchcraft."

"What about it?"

"Jesus Christ, how stupid could I be? It was right there and I was looking right at it and pretending that it couldn't happen. Wasn't I?"

"I suppose."

"I mean, you and David. And that detective. And Ginny. You killed Ginny, didn't you?"

"Not technically, no."

She hated it, but tears were starting at the edge of her eyes and Cheryl found herself breathing shallowly; her stomach felt nauseous. "He's not hurting you. There's nothing he could do to hurt you. But you want to kill him, don't you?"

He just looked at her.

"It's all this witchcraft shit, isn't it? The candles and that jewelry and everything."

He didn't say anything.

"Tell me, goddamn it! I have a right to know!"

Fry stood up.

"Oh, shit," Cheryl whispered.

"I want you to get down on the floor."

"I won't. You can't make me. You'll have to force me if—"

"I will if I have to."

"I'm not alone in this apartment building."

"You might as well be. Do you think anyone cares?"

"You just stay right there!"

"Miss D'Angelo, I want you to lie down on the floor. On your back. Bend your legs behind you. It'll be painful but you'll have to endure that."

"I won't do it."

"That way, if you try to move, you won't be able to. You'll be in a very awkward position. You see my point."

"I'm not going to do it."

"Yes. You are."

A few hours before dawn he reached Cheryl's apartment.

He was exhausted.

He pulled into the wide parking lot, drove past the cars on either side. He saw Cheryl's.

Farther down, nearly at the end of the lot, he saw Fry's.

Son of a bitch . . .

He turned his car around and headed back for the road.

Stopped for a moment and looked up at what he knew was the front window of Cheryl's apartment.

David couldn't see anything. The drapes were drawn. Lights were on.

Had he been there all night?

God, Cheryl . . .

He left.

Fry's house was dark, unlit, as David's car slid on the snow in front of it. Came to a stop.

He got out and looked around.

He looked across the lawn.

The dog.

The dog, the hellhound, the thing Fry had—what? Called down from the spirit world? Created from sticks and bones?

It saw him. It came loping across the lawn, red eyes dim lights in the darkness.

David heard the pounding of its paws, sensed the wave of energy from it as it came at him.

Faster than any real dog.

But he didn't get back into his car.

He stood where he was. Crossed his arms at the wrists.

"Come on, you son of a bitch . . ."

The red eyes huge, the noise of it solid, evil, elemental—

"Come on . . ."

It kicked up snow.

Growled.

Leaped.

Huge dog, all black, all jaws, red eyes, slavering, springing into the air and coming right at David—

"*Aeior!*"

Blue light.

For one moment the dog was brilliant and shimmering, bathed by the light.

And it never made a sound as its skeleton passed through the blue, as its skeleton, stripped of the earth and mud and soil and magic Fry had used to create it, dissolved.

The skeleton floated past David and clattered on the snowy driveway, smashed apart, bones and bits of bones flying into the air and skipping into the lawn.

Far away—from the other side—David heard its howl, its whining sorrow that faded, faded, and went quiet in the cold darkness.

He kicked in the front door, felt for the switch, and turned on the lights.

David expected an attack of some kind, so he was cautious. More dogs, or doors that opened into hell, or whispers of things from corners of darkness.

Things above him, ready to drop, shadows of jelly wrapping around him and suffocating him, dissolving his flesh.

The foyer was empty.

He turned right and went down the hall—very careful— and was seized for one moment by a kind of inner panic as a wave of cold moved through him. Sheer cold. But it passed as quickly as it had occurred, and he moved on.

Opened doors off the hall and looked in. Entered them and moved the furniture around, ripped up cushions, lifted rugs.

In the library he tore all the books from the shelves, scattered them and kicked them. Looked behind every hanging picture and tapestry as he ripped them down. Smashed the relics and statuettes and trophies Fry had collected from all over the world.

Goddamn it, it's here somewhere . . .

''Goddamn it, where is it? It's here, it's here!''

''David?''

''Oh, God, no . . .''

She was there. On the other side of the library. Half there. Her ghost, wandering, not seeing him.

"David, I'm so cold, I'm in pain."

"Ginny, no."

She walked through the furniture he had overturned.

"I can't see you, David. I'm in pain."

He knows I'm here, it's because he knows I'm here.

"Ginny!"

She turned and faced him. Held out a hand. "Help me, David!"

"Ginny, go away! It's not you! He's doing this!"

"Help me, David!"

Tears ran down her face. Ghost-tears. Then she laughed and sank to her knees. "It hurts, David!" She began to scream. A tentacle grew from her belly like some kind of birth. It wrapped between her legs and around her waist, curled around her throat.

"Ginny, it's not you! It's him!"

She fell to one side, struggling with the tentacle, and reached out for him again.

"I— David, the pain, the pain!"

"Leave her alone!" he screamed. "Leave her alone!"

Ginny laughed again, cackled, and was gone. Faded. Gone.

Swearing, David ran from the library.

And caught hold of himself.

Carefully, careful . . .

The dining room.

The kitchen.

Closets.

He looked in the obvious places first, then knocked over furniture, tore through cupboards, kicked the floorboards for a hollow space beneath.

And if he didn't find what he was after that way, then he'd start over again and tear the house apart, room by room, wall by wall, one nail at a time.

Back to the foyer. The foot of the stairs leading to the second floor.

"David? David . . ."

At the top of the stairs. She was bent over on hands and knees and a reptile, a demon, something, was behind her, bent over her, as if mating with her.

"David!"

He laughed. Laughed out loud. Maybe he was losing his mind, after all. But he started up the stairs, not hesitating, and when he came to his sister and the reptile they looked right at him, Ginny stuck out her tongue at him and wiped her lips lasciviously, the reptile smiled at him, and David walked right through them.

Again, that instant of cold, for only a moment.

On the second floor landing he didn't look back.

But the image was gone.

Fry's bedroom. He smashed the bureau, went through the closets, tore the bed apart, the mattress.

Spare rooms. Nothing.

The attic.

Here was where Fry had done his magic. It was warm in the attic, and David felt repercussions of pain, he could almost hear voices. Fry's. Long's. Ginny's voice, her real voice.

He knocked over tables, went through large wooden boxes filled with incense and candles, knives and bowls, books and more books—

Until finally he screamed.

"God, it's here somewhere! It's here! Where is it, you son of a bitch! *Where is it?*"

Furiously he picked up a chair and hurled it.

It smashed through the small oval window at the other end of the attic. Glass shattered. Cold air and snow blew in.

"Where is it, Fry?"

He was sweating, he was desperate, insane.

Maybe it wasn't here. Maybe it was with him? Maybe he kept it with him? Maybe it was in his car?

No, no, he wouldn't take that chance, it was too dangerous, the risk was too great, far too great.

It had to be *here.*

David walked across the shattered attic and sat down by the broken window in the cold air and the broken glass.

He wiped his face with his hands, breathed in the cold air.

Think, think . . .

He looked outside. The trees. The lawn. The sky was lightening, turning faintly gray. Almost dawn.

The trees—

"Oh, my God . . ."

A huge tree. An oak. In the side yard.

When he was a boy he'd sit inside that tree. It was his hiding place.

The snow began falling more heavily as David crossed the wide lawn and approached the oak.

It is *you, because it contains . . . everything you are. You must guard this book. Protect it.*

He stopped before the tree and crossed his arms.

"In nomine Agla Sabaoth Elohim, ite, spiritus malignos. Defende me, Enor et Ator."

He put out his right hand—

—his hand—

—carefully.

Feeling. For energy, for light, sound, anything.

"In nomine—"

The tree groaned. David felt warmth as he pushed his hand toward it, and the tree groaned as if touched by a heavy wind. Snow fell on him in heavy chunks, from the branches above him.

Water, melting snow, ran in rivers down the bark of the old oak, making it shine like a reptile's hide.

David stepped ahead and touched the tree.

It was very warm. Melted snow rained down on him, but he felt no shock, suffered no green light, no attack.

He stepped over thick wide roots, moving around the oak. It was hollow. A huge knot, decayed long ago, was like a mouth in the side of it. David reached inside.

Slowly.

Like reaching inside the petrified womb of some dead medieval witch.

"Defende me, in nomine Ator et Enor."

His fingers touched warmth. So deep that the sensation felt almost solid, jellylike or rubbery. But nothing alive. Nothing gripped his hand. He reached around.

Rain continued to drop on him. And shadows—

He looked up.

The heavy branches and limbs were moving down toward him. No wind. They were pulling toward him, curling down like arms, sensing him.

David smiled.

"Ite, ite, spiritus! Ator! Enor! Etor!"

They wavered, almost holding back. But continued to reach, closing down, feeling for him.

He searched blindly with his fingers—

Felt—

Felt it.

Brought it out.

It was wrapped in leather and tied with string. David backed away from the tree and knelt down in the snow and unwrapped it. A cold breeze blew upon him, and in the breeze the leather sheets fell to the ground and crawled away on the snow.

Fry's grimoire.

David opened it and scanned the pages. It was here, all here. A book of the dead. The spells created by Fry— spells by which a man might commit suicide and invoke himself to life again, reborn of a medieval demon.

And it was beautiful. Like something from a lost age. Heavy paper, colored ink. All done in hand, in Fry's hand. Lovingly done. A poem, a prayer.

Sorcery.

Resurrection.

Immortality.

An evil Christ, and not the figure David remembered from the seminary, not the figure he had sought long ago in penitence and guilt.

But a demon.

Cheryl was whimpering on the floor. "Let me roll over. Just let me—please—roll over! God, he's not coming, he's not coming . . ."

Fry rose to his feet. "Get up."

"Oh, Jesus, what're you going to do?"

"Get up!"

"David will be here!"

"Now!"

He was standing in the field. Right where Ginny had been found. David had drawn a circle around himself, dug it into the ground with a pocket knife. And in the center of the circle he'd cleared away the brown grass and built a small fire.

Above the trees to the east the sky was brightening, dark gray giving way to faint orange and yellow.

"In nomine Sabaoth, Spiritus Magnus . . ."

He waited, holding the grimoire.

He heard Fry's car when it pulled off the road and stopped in the field. He saw it, just beyond a line of low bushes. Watched as Fry, holding tightly to Cheryl, pushed her ahead of him.

Two shadows coming toward him across the field.

David picked up more small branches and dropped them into the fire. Sparks flew; the flames jumped higher.

"David!"

Her voice hit him hard. Her voice, and seeing her—Like this.

They came into the circle of light and Fry yanked Cheryl back so that she was pressed against him. He was holding her by her wrists, arms behind her back.

David could see Fry's face, see his eyes, behind Cheryl's blowing, tangled hair.

"What are you, priest?"

"A magician, like you. It truly does end here, Fry."

"Does it?"

"Let her go. Your having her won't stop me. This is between you and me."

"My battle is with the world."

"I'm the world tonight. And I'm sending you back to hell. Cheryl, walk away."

She struggled, but Fry had her. "David! He won't . . . let go!"

"I won't let go, priest. You must know how that feels."

"Let her go, Fry."

"When you're dead."

David opened the grimoire, randomly tore out several pages, and dropped them into the fire.

"Do that and I kill her. Then you."

David ripped out more pages, dropped them into the fire. Flames rose. Fry leaned his head away, moved his eyes behind Cheryl.

"Give me the book, priest!"

"David! What're you doing?"

"Give me the book, priest!"

"When you let her go!"

He tore out more pages and crumpled them, showed them to Fry, threw them into the building fire.

"You'll unleash hell!" Fry screamed at him.

"You're my hell! He's a dead man, Cheryl! He killed

himself! Then he brought himself back to life with this book! Only he's not a man! He's a demon! And he's trapped!''

"I'll kill her! Give me the book!''

More pages ripped, more pages thrown into the fire.

"This is for Emma! And Gray!''

Cheryl screamed. The hands holding her were tightening. And Fry—Fry was changing. Becoming warmer; becoming hot.

Thunder growled in the cold sky.

"This is for Long! And his wife!''

"I'll kill her!''

David looked up. The voice had changed. Not Fry's voice.

Cheryl screamed, "David! He's hurting me!''

Fry let go of her wrists and grabbed her by the head. A hand on each side.

Large hands. Less than human, now. Almost like paws.

Thunder boomed.

Demonic paws, to snap her neck.

"No more, priest! Give me the book!''

David watched Cheryl, stared into her eyes. Read my mind, read my mind . . .

He tore out another handful of pages, held them up—"For Ginny!''—and threw them in.

The fire hissed and the flames leaped high, brilliant.

Fry grunted and moved his head away.

"Now, Cheryl! Run!''

She moved.

But Fry twisted his hands quickly. There was a loud cracking noise.

"*No!*''

She was still looking at David as she fell, dropping forward limply, landing in the snow, sending up gusts of frost.

"*Fry!*''

"Give me the book, priest!"

A heavy wind blew down and more thunder boomed. David lifted the grimoire. Held it for Fry to see.

And brought it down, smashed it into the fire.

The flames blew high, sending ashes of the grimoire all across the field. Paper, leather, caught on fire and churned, curled.

Fry howled and staggered forward.

"Damn you back to hell!" David shrieked at him. "Bezemoth! *Bezemoth! Damn! You! Back! To! Hell-llll!*"

Fry shrieked. Inhuman. He pitched to one side, fell to the ground, stretched back. His body jumped convulsively.

He seethed, the flesh rotting away, the arms and legs curling and bending. His entire body quivered and twisted, crumpled—

Exploded.

Flesh and pieces of bone, rot and steam—

Thunder boomed.

The ground shook.

The wind tore at the flames of the fire.

And from Fry's shattered, splintered corpse erupted a flowing green mist. Swirling, collecting, forming itself into a shape, pulling itself into a rope of smoky light.

A rope of mist that pulled, pulled itself into the air, through the blowing snow, into the sky, swaying like a vine, climbing taller than the trees that surrounded the field.

Bezemoth.

It had features, far at the top of it. A dismal, lean, pointed face, half reptilian, half human. Something vague, barely able to hold itself together in the wind, on this world.

Snow and cold blew on David as he stared up at it. He didn't want to look at it; he closed his eyes against the snow.

The thunder boomed, and lightning, heat lightning, energy, shimmered above the trees. The dawn sky seemed to sway behind the demon as it writhed and floated.

"Ite!" David screamed at it. *"Ite! Bezemoth!"*

It hissed at him. It glowed.

And it spoke. Not in words. In sensations. Spoke in a voice that was not a voice but a song, melodious, beautiful.

Life is all. All is life. I can return her to you.

"No!" David yelled.

Teach you the words. All is life. Write the words.

"Ite! Ite, Bezemoth Ipsissimus! To hell!"

She is not dead. Life is all. Listen to the words.

It swayed in the wind, a tendril of green mist, something only David could see, something only David could hear.

You have burned the book. Listen to the words. In the names of Aszraoth and Sytry and Fel—

"No! *No!*" David closed his eyes, turned away, bent his head low and cupped his ears with his hands.

In the name of All That Is—

"No!" he screamed, facing it again, throwing up his arms, crossing them. "In nomine Sabaoth Elohim! *I* am the All! *I* am the Voice! Ite, Bezemoth Ipsissimus, ad locus vestrum!"

It hissed at him again, hissed in his brain, and swayed in the wind, coiled down to strike him.

As it came close, a curtain of blue light forced it back.

"Ite! Ite! Divina virtute infernum detrude! Ite!"

It reared back. Pulled itself higher.

Listen to the words—

"No-ooooo!"

And it began to dissolve. Too long in this world. Defeated. Broken from its house of flesh. Torn from its path. Fragmented by the wind and sucked higher into the sky, toward the stars, into—

Into the abyss, into the night beyond the stars, beyond the wind.

Life is all.

David sank to his knees and sobbed. Swallowed heavy, deep breaths of air.

What had he done?

The thunder fell quiet.

The ground steadied.

He looked up, and it was gone.

Looked across the field.

"Cheryl!"

He lifted his arms and called for protection.

"Guard me, in the name of Agla! Ite, omnes spiritus malignos!"

He crawled from the circle. Crawled on hands and knees. Crawled to Cheryl, touched her, looked at her, touched her face, her hair.

Rose to his feet and threw back his head and waved his fists wildly at the sky, at the wind, the snow and stars.

"No more death! Do you hear me? *No more death!*"

He began to cry.

"No more—death . . ."

He drew another circle, around Cheryl and himself.

Invoked his spirits.

Made the signs.

Held her head in his lap, stroked her hair, held her.

Looked high and made his invocation, called upon the spirits, his guardians, called upon—

Himself.

"I am the Bornless Spirit! I am the Voice! I am the Truth! I am the Earth and the Heavens! I am the Night and the Day! I am the Shadow and the Light!"

Around him came the blue wall of light, the cone of his universal energy, lifting toward the sky, beyond the sky.

"I am the Voice of All Things! I am the Born and the

Bornless! Earth and Fire! Air and Water! I am All That Is!''

The blue light colored his face, colored Cheryl's face. Radiant.

David looked up.

A Being . . . touched me. There was a mark.

Know . . . And believe.

The blue radiance faded, overcome by white.

Brilliant white. Pure white. Light so perfect and absolute that it was blinding, beyond color.

David looked down at Cheryl.

Beautiful. She was so beautiful, bathed in the perfect light of the All.

I am the Voice of All Things. I am All That Is.

Her nostrils quivered.

Her eyelids shuddered. Opened a little. Closed. Opened.

David felt behind her neck, her back. She was very warm.

She moaned and looked up at him, closed her eyes again quickly because of the brilliant light, but whispered his name.

He took her home, to his home, his house. She slept through the day and David sat by her, too exhausted to sleep. Watching her as she slept, afraid that somehow he had done something false or untrue or unnatural, that she would slip away from him again.

She woke up in the evening and ate some soup. David had some with her. But it was a dream, and she slept again, and David went to sleep with her, through the night.

The next morning he told her what had happened.

Cheryl couldn't remember anything about it. Only Fry behind her, holding her head. And the next moment, waking up in David's arms. The rest—vague shapes.

"Was I—? I was really . . . dead?"

"Nothing dies. Nothing ever really dies."

But what had once filled him with wonder and hope and illumination now seemed dreadful.

Nothing ever really dies.

Cheryl didn't go to work. She and David packed fresh clothes for him, then went to her apartment, where they put some of her things into a suitcase.

David went in first, walked into her apartment first, because the sense of violation that she felt, the fear, was still there. But it was her apartment; nothing had changed.

She made lunch and they watched "News at Noon." There was coverage of a horribly burned body found in a field outside the city. Police were investigating.

David tried to phone Emma, to tell her that they were coming, but there was no answer.

They left early in the afternoon.

He and Cheryl didn't speak much during the drive but occasionally they held hands, and when they looked each other in the eyes, they knew. They knew.

Cheryl had brought along Ginny's diary and she read it and reread it. Asked David about the Celestial Alphabet.

What does it really say? I asked Fry and he said it was trivial.

"What does it really say, David?"

"It's about . . . the things they did. Ginny and Fry. Their ceremonies. Trying to reach Mom and Dad. She was in love with him."

"Was she?"

"As much in love as anybody can be, and still be wrong about it."

"Poor Ginny."

"It's her grimoire. Not like Fry's, but a start. She was trying, only she didn't understand. Part of her soul is in this book. If I'd known that then, maybe I could've changed things."

Cheryl looked at him.

"It's the things you don't know until it's too late," David said.

Late in the evening he pulled up the steep driveway of Emma's house. He and Cheryl got out of the car.

"Fry did this?" Cheryl asked.

"Fry did this."

David stepped up onto the porch.

There was an envelope tacked to the door, addressed to him. David took it down, stepped off the porch, and walked back toward the car.

"What is it? David?"

He got into the car and left his door open so he could read by the dome light. Cheryl came in and sat beside him, and as David finished each page he handed it to Cheryl so that she could read it, as well.

Dear David,

I know what has happened. I've felt it. You have done something great and profound. You've restored the balance and cleansed the earth of a great evil. But I know you know that.

I have a confession to make. When you came to me I knew that you were gifted and I wanted to believe— yes! believe!—that in the order and purpose of Life what Ted had done could somehow be corrected. I could not do it. Gray was too full of guilt and regret—I'm sure you guessed that Gray was the one who originally taught Ted. Evil is very simple in its power and very seductive. It promises small things at first. Gray and I made mistakes.

I have learned a great lesson. A very painful lesson. Do you realize that when you love deeply, you sometimes unleash terrible things? Be very careful of that. Evil always begins with the best of intentions. Whatever we do has consequences. That was the purpose of our teaching you, but it is something that I think you already know.

There is one more thing. I want you to know that I think of you as the son I never had. Remember that everyone has parents—parents who bring them into the world and give them life, and parents who give them spiritual life. So I think of you as our child—mine and Ted's.

We have given you spiritual life.

You possess a great gift and you will be a stranger in this world. You must not presume to be wise. And remember that you are never truly alone.

I'm sorry that I will not meet Cheryl, but in a way I have met her, because I know you.

It is best that I do this, for reasons I know you'll understand.

Dominus vobiscum, magus.

And—love—

Emma

She was in the sitting room, lying on the couch. She'd left a light on. The empty bottle was on the floor beside her.

David turned his head away. Wiped his eyes. Looked at her again.

Cheryl came in; the letter trembled in her hand. "She was a beautiful woman."

David whispered, "Dominus vobiscum, magistra."

And made a sign in the air.

He buried her on a small hill in the back yard, next to the grave Emma had made for Gray. Cheryl watched David but did not help.

He prayed as he did it.

And he didn't mark the grave. No cross, no headstone.

David wanted to put flowers on the soil of Emma's grave because she had always loved flowers, but there were none, now. It was late autumn and the earth was brown and gray and the sky cold and close.

But he took a talisman—one that Emma had made for him downstairs in the workshop—and he placed it just under the earth of her grave.

He did the same for Gray.

And in the middle of the night he placed a brass bowl on each of their graves and filled them with incense and lit the incense.

He prayed over the burning incense.

He did not ask God to forgive them. There is no God; we are God; life is all. There is nothing to forgive.

He did not mourn what they had accomplished in life, for life is ceaseless, and whatever has been done has been done. There is no need to mourn what one has done in life, no need to mourn birth and life and experience, no need to mourn laughter, anticipation, sorrow, vengeance, anger, want, desire, mystery.

But David thanked Emma and Gray. For through them he had learned. Life is all. There is nothing that is not life. They had brought him change and insight and knowledge and true humility. They had given him himself, newly born, awake, whole.

When he was done he made the last signs over their graves and bowed over each one. Then he came down the hill.

Cheryl asked him carefully, "Is that how magicians have their funerals?"

"Yes, that's how."

"It's lovely, David."

He asked her if she would get Ginny's diary from the car. Cheryl did so.

David carried it into the grass and set it down, opened

it, crossed his arms over his chest and whispered a prayer over it.

Then he set it on fire.

"David!" Cheryl called from the driveway.

He walked back to her.

"Why?"

"Because she's all right, now."

"Ginny's all right?"

"Yes."

She took his hand and they watched until the fire had burned itself out.

"Ginny's safe, now," Cheryl said, gripping his hand strongly.

"Nothing dies," he told her. "Nothing ever really dies."

In Noland, Ohio, a blanket of snow covered Theodore Fry's house. It sat in darkness, black, a monolith.

The wind blew through it because windows had been smashed and its front door broken in.

But it was silent and dead.

Thunder boomed above it.

Lightning, very far away in the cold sky, flashed slowly.

Upstairs, a light flickered. A light in the attic.

Flickered, feebly trying to stay alive.

Flickered—

And went out.

Avon Books presents your worst nightmares—

...haunted houses

ADDISON HOUSE   75587-4/$4.50 US/$5.95 Can
Clare McNally

THE ARCHITECTURE OF FEAR
                      70553-2/$3.95 US/$4.95 Can
edited by Kathryn Cramer & Peter D. Pautz

...unspeakable evil

HAUNTING WOMEN   89881-0/$3.95 US/$4.95 Can
edited by Alan Ryan

TROPICAL CHILLS   75500-9/$3.95 US/$4.95 Can
edited by Tim Sullivan

...blood lust

THE HUNGER   70441-2/$4.50 US/$5.95 Can
THE WOLFEN   70440-4/$4.50 US/$5.95 Can
Whitley Strieber

JAMES ELLROY

Author of *The Black Dahlia* and *The Big Nowhere*
"*Echoes the Best of Wambaugh*"
New York Sunday News

BROWN'S REQUIEM   78741-5/$3.95 US $4.95 Can
Join ex-cop and sometimes P.I. Fritz Brown beneath the golden glitter of Tinsel Town...where arson, pay-offs, and porn are all part of the game.

CLANDESTINE   81141-3/$3.95 US /$4.95 Can
Nominated for an Edgar Award for Best Original Paperback Mystery Novel. A compelling thriller about an ambitious L.A. patrolman caught up in the sex and sleaze of smog city where murder is the dark side of love.

SILENT TERROR   89934-5/$3.50 US /$4.75 Can
Enter the horrifying world of a killer whose bloody trail of carnage baffles police from coast to coast and whose only pleasure is to kill...and kill again.

FEATURING LLOYD HOPKINS

BLOOD ON THE MOON   69851-X/$3.95 US /$4.95 Can
Lloyd Hopkins is an L.A. cop. Hard, driven, brilliant, he's the man they call in when a murder case looks bad.

"A brilliant detective and a mysterious psychopath come together in a final dance of death."
The New York Times Book Review

BECAUSE THE NIGHT   70063-8/$3.50 US /$4.95 Can
Detective Sergeant Lloyd Hopkins had a hunch that there was a connection between three bloody bodies and one missing cop...a hunch that would take him to the dark heart of madness...and beyond.

WHITLEY STRIEBER

THE #1 BESTSELLER
COMMUNION
70388-2/$4.95 US/$5.95 Can

A NOVEL OF TERROR BEYOND YOUR IMAGINING
THE WOLFEN
70440/$4.50 US/$5.95 Can

THE ULTIMATE NOVEL OF EROTIC HORROR
THE HUNGER
70441-2/$4.50 US/$5.95 Can

and coming soon

TRANSFORMATION

The world will never be the same...

Zecharia Sitchin's
The Earth Chronicles

BOOK I: THE 12TH PLANET
39362-X/$4.95 US/$6.50 CAN

This revolutionary work brings together lost, antediluvian texts, ancient cosmologies, and newly discovered celestial maps to reach the shocking conclusion that we are descendants of a superior race from the 12th planet.

BOOK II: THE STAIRWAY TO HEAVEN
63339-6/$4.95 US/$6.50 CAN

The mysteries of man's pursuit of immortality and after-life with the gods is researched through the astounding conclusions based on names, places, and monuments whose true meanings have been lost for centuries.

BOOK III: THE WARS OF GODS AND MEN
89585-4/$4.95 US/$5.95 CAN

Mankind's earliest records reveal a startling new theory of human origins—and of the "gods" who destroyed the first civilization!